Killing Gravity

D1007994

KILLING GRAVITY

COREY J. WHITE

A TOM DOHERTY ASSOCIATES BOOK

NEW YORK

KILLING GRAVITY

Copyright © 2017 Corey J. White

Cover illustration by Tommy Arnold
Cover design by Christine Foltzer

Edited by Carl Engle-Laird

A Tor.com Book
Published by Tom Doherty Associates
175 Fifth Avenue
New York, NY 10010

www.tor.com

Tor® is a registered trademark of
Macmillan Publishing Group, LLC.

ISBN 978-0-7653-9508-5 (ebook)
ISBN 978-0-7653-9631-0 (trade paperback)

First Edition: May 2017

For Ella

Killing Gravity

CHAPTER ONE

Trying to comprehend a whole star system while my ship bleeds atmosphere? There are worse ways to die.

Control panels glow in fuchsia panic. Low steady hiss of oxygen. I'm floating in what used to be the cockpit of the battered Oxeneer-class corvette I called home these past few years. Now it's a coffin with ambient lighting, adrift in the void.

Seven crawls into my helmet and gets fur up my nose. I feel like I'm being smothered but can't get too angry with her; she probably just wants to make sure I'm still breathing. With Seven blocking my mouth, the condensation on the inside of my helmet starts to clear. I can see out the viewport, where the local system has pulled out all the stops. One bright star and five planets hang in space, with a shimmering silver sphere just off the bow, orbited by debris. All these celestial bodies look carefully arranged, like they're trying to tell me something.

Fuchsia flicks over to light blue as a message comes through the comms.

```
Distress Signal Response. Assistance incom-
ing. T-minus thirteen minutes.
```

The words come across the inside of my helmet. There's more, but Seven is in the way, purring gently. And, anyway, trying to focus on the glowing letters makes the pain behind my right eye worse. My head pulls to the left of its own volition, the way it does when I've got a migraine, and I get even more of Seven's fur in my nose.

They're probably all ruined, but I disable security countermeasures and watch the slow ballet of planets through the viewport while I wait, trying to ignore the ache in my head. The speckled purple planet in the middle drifts out of sync with the others, and for a second I'm sure it's telling me to run.

An echoing *doozh* sounds through the ship, and my heart rate spikes so high that my Head-Up Display flashes a warning—as though a pulsing red exclamation mark is going to help me relax.

I hear the sound of cutters working on the hull; with the docking mechanism trashed, they have to cut their way in. This will play out one of two ways: either it's a legit rescue, or they're leeching me. They'll pull away with a circular chunk of my hull, spilling my remaining atmosphere into the void, then they'll wait until suffocation or the cold kills me.

I leave the cockpit, headed for the sound of their cutters, stopping in the armory on the way through.

• • •

The Klaxon sounds and my heart jumps again. I'm just waiting for the hull to be cut away and reveal the depths of space beyond. Instead, it splits down the middle and I see the external door of the other ship. The light over the air lock starts spinning, and as I watch it I try to calm my breathing so it matches the cycle of its spin. Inhale two full rotations, exhale two full rotations.

The panel beside the air lock pings and turns green, and the door opens silently.

The woman standing in the doorway is tall and broad, held upright by her ship's gravity while I'm stuck floating. She's the palest person I've seen in a long time, so pale her blond hair might actually be natural. It's cropped military-short under the helmet of her suit, and her back is proper rigid. Her silhouette is made even larger by the fierce-looking combat exoskeleton bolted to her limbs and torso.

"You alone?" she asks. Her voice sounds tinny over the thinband universal comms.

The scattergun in her hands looks even more dangerous than she does. She could have brought a waver—a tight-beam neutron blast that destroys organic matter and not much else—but I figure the heavy weaponry is a message. She's telling me she's only here because they're legally required to respond to a distress beacon. If I want to mess about, she'll have no qualms putting me down.

"Just me and Seven," I say. She looks at me quizzically, and Seven yawns and stretches inside my helmet. If I hadn't just danced with that bounty hunter, I'd twist her exoskeleton into a pretty figurehead for the front of her ship, but I can barely keep both eyes open with the pain in my head.

"I need a retinal scan before I let you on board," she says. That's when I notice the drone hovering over her shoulder—a lensed metal ball, the air surrounding it distorted by its miniature propulsion drive.

"I don't think you should do that."

"Rather I leave you here? 'Cause that's the only other option."

My hand reaches for the plasma charges in my satchel, but I stop myself, then sigh. "You do what you've gotta do."

The drone hovers over and flashes a light in my eye, and instantly my migraine peaks again. My head pulls to the left, and to her it probably looks like I'm trying to dodge the scan.

The little drone blips happily, and the soldier looks at

her wrist-mounted screen. "Mariam Xi," she says, and I let her pronounce it wrong.

"Just Mars," I say.

"There's very little about you in the system."

"I like to keep my nose clean."

"Yeah, or the opposite," she says. "Einri, scan the rest of the ship for life-forms, weapons, anything worth its weight in creds."

Everything I care about is in my suit and my satchel. They can have the rest. They *will* have the rest; emergency response might be mandatory under imperial law, but that doesn't mean it's free.

"Come aboard then, *Mars*." She says it like I'd lie about my own name, like she doesn't even trust me that far. She's smarter than she looks.

• • •

The first one to greet me after we cycle through the air lock is the AI.

"Welcome aboard the *Nova*," it says, voice flat. It's not so much androgynous as completely artificial. Most ship owners splurge on a personality module, so whoever runs this ship must be very cheap, very biz, or very both.

"What *is* the *Nova*?" I ask.

"The *Nova* is an Easter-class crusher and tug," the AI

informs me. "Built out of the Otomo-Ward shipyards in—"

"That's plenty, ship." I've never jacked a tug before, but I can see how it might have its upsides.

"It's called Einri," a new voice says. "I'd appreciate it if you showed the AI an atom of respect."

"My bad," I say, then offer them a small smile. I guess this person must be the captain and owner. They aren't always one and the same, but without any corporate insignia in the main hold, I assume it's a small operation.

The captain is tall, slender, with soft-looking lips on an otherwise sharp face. The clothing is all shades of gray—large, flat panels of fabric cut into an angular jacket and long skirt. It's a deliberately gender-neutral ensemble, the sort of thing some people might miss or deliberately ignore, but one that I'm plenty familiar with. Their feet are bare, and they must be following my gaze, because their toes curl against the textured metal floor.

I can feel the bulk of the soldier standing behind me, and the captain nods to her. She waits a few long seconds before she moves past me, exoskeleton clanking against the floor. She puts the scattergun in a locker along the far wall and makes a show of locking and palm-printing it before leaving the hold.

Once we're alone, the captain asks, "What are you planning to do with your ship?"

I shrug. "Nothing; it's scrap."

"Scrap's my specialty." They smile now, because this emergency response might actually be worth something at the end of the day. "What about the other, ah, object?"

I don't want to explain what it used to be and how it got into its current spherical situation, so instead I say, quietly, "I don't think anyone's gonna claim that wreckage."

They hold out a hand and I start to freak out: Do they expect money? Or an ID pass? Then after I've stared at the hand for way too long, I remember. I unclasp the lock on my suit's gauntlet, take it off, and shake their hand.

"You can call me Squid," they say. Now that I'm looking closely at their face I see a flow of color beneath the skin. They must see me staring, because the chromatophores change to a soft shade of pink, like reddening cheeks, responding to stimulus.

"I'm Mars."

"It's a pleasure, Mars. As per imperial regulation, you're entitled to food and board until we reach our next port, and I'm entitled to charge you for same. I can deduct it, and my rescue fee, from the creds earned after selling your ship for scrap, or you can work to pay your way."

"The deduct thing—let's go with that," I say, running out of words as quickly as I'm running out of energy. I feel Seven scurrying inside my suit and rushing down my arm. She sticks her head out of the sleeve and looks around, slitted eyes taking in the dock.

"Delightful," Squid says, then reaches down.

I expect a squeal, but Seven doesn't bite. She gives Squid's proffered hand a quick sniff, then runs up the extended arm to perch on their shoulder.

"What is it?" Squid asks and scratches under Seven's chin; she leans into it.

"I dunno; some sort of experiment. I rescued her when I was a kid," I say, which is totally, technically, true.

Squid glances at me, then back to Seven. "When you were a kid?"

Seven suddenly decides she's bored with this new human and jumps, but it's only a short drop and she doesn't need to flaunt her glide membrane just yet.

Squid looks like they're about to ask me something else.

"If you don't mind," I sputter out, "I think I'd like to bunk down. Catastrophic systems failures tend to take it out of a girl, not to mention floating in the abyss waiting to die. Maybe just wake me for the next meal?"

"Yes, that's fine. Einri will guide you to your quarters. Do you need anything from your ship before it's crushed?"

I just shake my head and walk away; I get the feeling

that Squid could extend this conversation indefinitely. I make a clicking noise in the back of my throat, and Seven scampers up from wherever she's been sniffing about to climb up onto my shoulder.

Quarters are close to the dock, and it only takes a couple of minutes of following Einri's directions to get there. I drop my satchel, strip out of the rest of my space suit, and lay down. I swear I'm out before my head hits the pillow.

CHAPTER TWO

"I'd really prefer if you didn't do that." Squid's voice sounds a bit odd, and when I glance up I see it's because they're talking to me via the ship's minidrone, its lens-eye looking down at me.

The three plasma charges are laid out on the floor and I'm crouching down, trying to remember the passcode I used to lock the detonator. "Uh, this isn't what it looks like," I say, not sounding very convincing.

"So you weren't planning a one-woman shipjacking?"

Shit.

"We need to talk, Mars; everyone's gathering in the mess hall. If you pack those charges away and head to the mess now, this little misunderstanding can stay between the two of us. Otherwise, I send Trix to come find you. Believe me when I say she won't take your explosive plot as calmly as I have."

Talk? I don't know what Squid's game is, but any rational captain would have me ejected out the nearest air lock.

"All right, let's talk." I stand up, and the drone starts

moving down the hallway, gliding backward so it can keep its eye on me.

When I get to the mess hall, everyone is already waiting for me—but by "everyone" I just mean Squid, the soldier Trix, and some other guy. I expected a tug to need more manpower, but I guess the ship and its AI must do most of the work. Now that Trix is out of the space suit, I see one of her arms is prosthetic—the same glossy black and deep red as the exoskeleton she was wearing.

"Oh, hey," the guy says, lifting a forkful of rehydrated egglike protein to his mouth. He nods at me; his head is close-shaved, skin glossy beneath the mess-hall lights. He's got a broad frame, but there isn't much of him hanging off it.

Trix just scowls at me, and for a second I think Squid told her about the bombs, but then I figure if that was the case, she'd do a lot more than scowl. Squid's at the far end of the mess, pacing.

"So, what's this about, Squid?" I say.

"We have company inbound—an imperial vessel. We've been ordered to stay here and await their arrival."

"How did they find us?" the guy asks.

"I told you not to scan me," I say to Trix, and for a split second her brow furrows. That look tells me she thought they were coming for *her,* and all of a sudden Trix gets a little more interesting in my books.

She stands and her chair tips over. "You brought this down on us?" she says, but it's less a question and more an accusation. She charges at me, and without the exoskeleton she moves fast—too fast. Before I can stop her, she's got her massive paw of a hand wrapped around my throat.

I can feel my face turning red, but I give her a cheeky grin; in my experience, when someone's acting tough, nothing pisses them off more.

"Let go of her, Trix," Squid says.

"How about instead I snap her neck?" She clenches her prosthetic fist, and I don't doubt the arm could do it.

"Trix, trust me."

Trix loosens her grip, and that's when I strike out. She flies backward and lands on the mess-hall table, scattering food and ersatz coffee. The guy jumps out of the way, saying, "What the hell?" but then he's leaning down over Trix, checking on her.

Squid walks across the room. "There's no need for that," they say, hands up placating-like, as though I'm an angry animal or a kid throwing a tantrum. "You're among friends here."

"Like hell she is," Trix says, picking herself up off the table.

"Trix," Squid barks, angry and impatient. They stare Trix down, playing the boss card, which Trix seems to grudgingly respect. After holding their gaze for a long moment, Trix looks away and Squid continues. "There's plenty of room on this ship, plenty of work, and we could use someone with your talents."

At least now I know why Squid is trying to stay on my good side. Though I do wonder how they figured it out.

"The only *talents* she's shown are sleeping and bringing trouble down on us," Trix says, but she sounds uncertain, and I'm guessing my little telekinetic display unsettled her.

Before Squid can say anything, Einri interrupts. "Excuse me, captain. There's a gravitational field forming within dangerous proximity of the *Nova*."

"Take evasive action."

Einri doesn't respond with words, but I feel the ship shift beneath my feet, and the pull of gravity deep in my gut.

"We'll have to pick up this family meeting later," Squid says, then they turn and run toward the cockpit.

• • •

I can hear Squid's soft footfalls ahead of me, but I'd probably still lose them if it wasn't for Einri's directions. Without a personality mod, it's hard to say, but I'm pretty sure it's pissed at me. I would be, too, if someone had been planning to rig my guts with explosives.

I get to the cockpit and I'm actually impressed. It's way more advanced than the utilitarian, scuffed metal of the rest of the ship: modular control panels, with screens on every surface giving a near-360-degree view of the surround.

I wait for Squid to do something, then I see their rigid posture and the blank look in their eyes and I realize they already are doing something—a pilot suite implant is giving them direct access to all systems. I'm so impressed I nearly whistle.

"You mind letting me in on your neural chatter?" I ask.

"Sorry," Squid says, except they don't actually say it: the voice comes from the room itself.

"The wormhole's gravitational differential is low," Einri says, "well within standard operating limits. It's only the proximity that's a factor."

"How long do we have?"

Before Einri can respond, we get the answer. The ship emerges from a wormhole on our starboard side, folding down into its fourth-dimensional form, planes and vertices being spat out by the universe itself. A wormhole always brings some gravity from its starting point—the bigger the differential between start and end points, the more likely you're going to cause some major damage.

"*Wolf-Spider*, armored personnel frigate," Einri says.

What Einri *doesn't* say is that it's got the MEPHISTO colors painted down its side—no logos, *that'd* be too obvious. At this distance we can't see yet, but shocktroopers will already be scurrying out onto the hull with their tensile tethers and weldthrowers, preparing to launch at the *Nova* as soon as they're in range.

"The scrapped ship floating nearby when we found you—was that connected to this?" Squid asks.

So that's how Squid figured it out: ran some scans on the ball of wreckage I made.

"Not officially, but yeah, probably," I say, and I realize it must sound really vague. I feel bad bringing this kind of heat down on them, right as they caught me planning a shipjacking, no less. "It's a long fucking story."

"Einri's been playing dumb with the comms panel since that first message came through, but if they get troops on board, I'll have to cooperate."

"I know, I know," I say. "How do I get to the air lock?"

"What are you going to do?"

"I'm gonna take care of it. How do I get to the air lock?"

"Can you promise me you won't try and steal my ship if we help you?"

I just nod, and then I remember that Squid's oculars are probably busy with operational data. "Yeah, I won't try it again; you have my word."

"Einri, show her the way, and find us a wormhole."

• • •

The guy is standing naked in the vestibule, the pants half of his space suit pooled around his ankles. I stand in the doorway for a few seconds, not really sure where to look, unable to stop myself from seeing the way he has absolutely no hair on his body. In the mess hall I just thought his head was razored, but it's more than that. I can even see his weird, hairless ball-sack dangling between his legs.

He bends down to pull up his pants, and that's when I finally look away. He holds the pants with one hand, turns around, and offers his other. "Mookie."

I shake it. "Mars."

Each of his forearms is decorated with a luminescent tattoo—fine lines that shimmer and glow above the skin. One is a caduceus, the other the schematics for some model of rifle. On his upper arm there's a patch of pinkish skin, glossy like plastic, and I figure that's where his unit insignia would have been. When you sign up to the imperial military—or are drafted—they put you through a process they call Temporary Augmented Alopecia. You go AWOL and you're stuck that way for life. Some vets prefer to stay hairless after living like that for a few years;

makes them feel like they're still connected, I guess, still part of the service.

"You don't need to come out with me," I say.

"You're not the only one with a dog in this race."

I put my satchel down, and Seven pokes her head out and stares at me. "Stay on board," I say, "this won't take long." She runs up my body, coming to rest on my shoulder. I sigh. "All right then."

After I've suited up we pass through the air locks. As we leave the exterior door the artificial gravity releases its hold. I drift outside, and my eyes want to look out to the stars, but I force them down to the hull of the ship so I can see the handholds.

I left my hooded cloak on underneath the space suit for Seven, because it's better than her blocking half my view while I fend off a boarding party. Already I can feel her purring against my spine; she could sleep anywhere.

"Einri, can you spin the ship around; give us a clear view?" Mookie asks.

"Negative. Locating a wormhole takes navigational precedence."

We clamber around the hull fast, or as fast as one can in zero gravity. First a large orange planet comes into view, its surface obscured by gray-black clouds, then the *Wolf-Spider* is there, stars twisting and blurred in the wake of its engines.

From the ship's-eye-view it looked small and distant, but now seeing the frigate proper, my heart is thundering. Like all imperial vessels, MEPHISTO ships are Northern Cooperative designs; the hull's curved surfaces make them look grown as much as built—biological, insectoid. Where an insect's eyes would be are a hundred lenses and other sensors, and its carapace bristles with spikes that could be antennae or weaponry. *I hope they still want me alive.*

This close I can see the shocktroopers on the ship's hull—burgundy smudges shimmering against the background of space. I hook my tether to the hull and wait.

Mookie comes up beside me, and through his visor I can see his facial tattoos glowing in the dim light of space. He takes hold of the waver that dangles from his belt, then asks, "What do you need me to do?"

"Drag me inside if I pass out."

"Huh?"

I ignore him because the *Wolf-Spider* has started banking. The first squad launches, and I focus on the trooper to the far right. I sweep my hand across, and they tumble sideways, spinning. The shocktroopers are all tethered together—I send the whole pack plunging left and down away from us, a tangle of bodies and tensile steel.

"Void-damned spacewitch," Mookie says, breathless.

He sounds impressed rather than freaked out, but still

I say, "Don't fucking call me that."

The first squad is already retracting when the second blasts off from the personnel launch pads. I make a shoving motion, and they go backward, spinning head over ass until they collide with other soldiers on the hull.

I don't *have* to move my hands, but it helps focus my intention, pushing body and mind to one purpose. That's what they taught us, anyway, when I was a kid. I can feel my brain inside my skull—not a pain, just a presence. No matter how many times I do this, I can never get used to it. It's like my brain is vibrating in there, or swelling up against the bone. It feels wrong. It feels like I was born for this.

They must think I could do this all day, because the next group are a pack of specialists, launching off the hull with personal blastpacks, white hiss of gas escaping behind them and no tethers to get tangled in.

I yell, loud, forcing the sound up from my diaphragm—another trick they taught us—and swat these elite troops one by one. By the time they're all spinning off into space, my throat is on fire.

"You fucks!" I sweep my arm out, and the troopers on the hull scatter, bouncing off the hull and stopping suddenly at the ends of their tethers. I feel that pressure building up in my chest and pause. I exhale and I force myself to remember these aren't the same troops, these aren't the ones who were there; maybe they don't deserve to die. *Maybe.*

The *Wolf-Spider* spins again and banks up, revealing a series of tubes along its base. A missile shoots toward the *Nova*'s engines, and I reach out and grab it. I think about sending it back and killing every last one of those troopers, but I don't. I crush the missile in my hand, and the explosion must be like a declaration of war, because more missiles tear through the void between ships, and I fling them away from the *Nova*.

I'm screaming again and Seven is awake now. She's in the helmet with me, and she's baring her tiny little teeth at the whole universe like she's going to kill it herself, like together we'll watch it all burn. And there's water building up in my eyes, and the missiles look like blurry stars streaking through space, and all I want to do is die and kill and cry, and then my vision shrinks down to a single pixel, and I know what that means, but it's too late to stop it.

CHAPTER THREE

I open my eyes and Squid is sitting over me. I turn my head and see Mookie, holding a needle.

"No fucking needles." I squirm away from him and it hurts, but I hold a hand out ready to throw him against the wall.

"Relax," he says, putting the needle down. "If you don't like needles, best not to look at your left hand." I'm about to tear at the drip I guess is stuck into the back of my hand, but he says, "You need fluids; just forget it's there and I'll take it out when you're ready."

I ignore him and try to glance down, but Seven is curled up asleep on my chest and I can't see over her. *Cute little jerkface.*

"I was expecting another sphere," Squid says.

"Wasn't sure I felt like killing that many people." I can feel the headache building already. "You couldn't have scavenged it anyway."

"I know that," Squid says, "I just wanted to watch it happen. You know this ship is a crusher, right?"

"Yeah, Einri said so."

"Well, you crushed that other vessel tighter than the *Nova* could have. I had Einri's drones scan it, to try and figure out what it was and whose remains were smeared across the inside."

I can't help but chuckle at that. "Bounty hunter," I say; "tracked me for months."

"Why'd they want you so bad?" Trix says. I turn my head and see her leaning in the doorway, prosthetic arm crossed over her organic one. "First a bounty hunter, now a void-damned troop carrier?"

I roll my eyes. "Maybe the rest of you like sitting around the viewport telling stories and holding hands, but that ain't me."

I try to roll over, but Seven digs her claws into my chest for purchase and I have to roll back.

Mookie gets up, and I watch him walk to the door and put his hand around Trix's waist. "Come on, we'll let her rest."

Trix glares at me for another second, then they leave.

After a pause I say to Squid, "There must be twenty years between them."

"If you aren't telling stories, then neither am I." They get up to leave, pausing in the door. "My offer still stands, if you want to join us. If not, we're on the edge of Eridani now, and we'll be at Aylett Station in a couple of days; you can disembark there and find your own way."

They leave before I can start to answer. *After every-thing, Squid still wants me on board?* I'm not sure if that's brave or dumb. But I've got contacts on Aylett—not friends exactly, but familiar faces at least.

I move my left hand and feel the tug of tubing, and I have to exhale deeply to push the image of my punctured skin out of my mind. I move my right hand instead and start stroking Seven, rubbing along her jawline.

People have tried to tell me she looks like a cat, but tiny. Cats come from Terra, and as far as I know, cats can't squeeze their whole bodies through gaps only big enough for their heads. They definitely can't glide through the air on skin membranes.

I clasp her against my chest, stand up, and walk over to the viewport, dragging the fluid pod behind me. Seven climbs to my shoulder and we both stare out into space, counting stars.

CHAPTER FOUR

Every station has its own smell, depending on what kind of plants they use to make the oxygen, and what brand of scrubbers. They use ferns on Aylett, so the whole place has a sweet and earthy scent—a smell you can feel tingling your nose hairs. I fucking hate it.

"You won't reconsider?" Squid asks.

They've followed me out into the bay, pretending like it's to oversee the unloading of the scrap they're hauling, but we both know Einri can handle that on its own.

"Look, I appreciate you reaching out or whatever, but I've got my own shit going on."

"Maybe we can help."

"Or maybe you'll die trying. I don't need that on my conscience."

"If you change your mind, we're going to be here for at least a day; got a long haul out to the Periphery, so I'll be haggling ruthlessly for supplies."

They hold out their hand and I shake it.

"Best of luck," they say.

"Thanks; you too."

I walk away, heading through the pallets, containers, and smaller vessels parked in the loading bay. I can feel Squid watching me leave, and I'm sure there's another pair of eyes too—probably Trix's, making sure I've actually gone.

I fish Seven out from the hood of my cloak, stash her in my satchel, then pull the hood up over my head. I strap a rebreather over my face to hinder station surveillance. As a bonus it cuts out most of the fern smell.

The dock is off-limits to surveillance because the transport union is crooked as shit and needs privacy to do its dodge, but as soon as I walk out, it starts: mounted cameras in every corner of the ceiling and floor, surveillance drones flitting through the air, the occasional squeal of feedback when two audio snoopers get too close.

I hock the plasma charges and detonator and get royally screwed, but a few creds is better than a free forfeit at the weapons checkpoint. Hock anything *other* than weapons outside the checkpoints and you deserve to be ripped off.

I skip the first couple of banks of vertilators, weighed down as they are with workers, tourists, and the odd newly married triple or couple. They flock to Aylett because it's lousy with casinos, as well as the hotels and resorts that feed on casinos like mold on damp. Down the far end of the causeway are the vertilators I need—the ones scrawled with graf and spattered with the thick frogspawn of dried spit.

FOR A GOOD TIME, CALL THE EMPERER
GROUNDWELLERS, FUCK OFF!
LIFE IS WHAT HAPPENS ON SOME PLANET WHILE
YOUR STUCK HERE

I hit the panel for Ring One and grab on to the hand-hold as the vertilator drops me through a couple hundred meters of artificial gravity.

• • •

Beneath Ring One is Zero, but it isn't called *Ring* Zero, because it isn't a ring. It's a spherical cavern housing the reactor that powers the whole station. They must figure it's safer in the center, and they get to pump waste heat through the joint for free heating.

I pull the rebreather off my face and leave it hanging around my neck. The smell of humanity is thick enough down here to cover the fern smell, but it's still its own kind of unpleasant.

Ring One is where my people live. Well, not *my* people, but the closest thing I want to find: the freaks, the runaways, the perpetual wanderers, the organized crime, the genehackers, the bodychoppers, the digital-wannabes, the loose, the inebriated, the ones with no common sense, no career and no desire for one, the fed up, fucked up, and flamed out. The whole place is like a dangerous chemical concoction. You never know what might set off a reaction, and the threat of violence hangs in the air thick as the smell.

The main problem with being around my people is that I hate people. Spend enough time alone, and being surrounded by people is the least natural thing you can imagine; it's like I can feel my psyche itch. Murmuring voices flood over me, and my lungs burn like I'm struggling to breathe through their massed exhalations.

My fight-or-flight response is kicking in hard as I push through the throng, and I'm starting to get a headache from the way my eyes dart left and right looking for incoming danger. They're not looking low, though, so Seven's hissing is my only hint that a prepubescent pickpocket is trying to rob me. I turn around just in time to see a small hand disappear back into the crowd, caked in dirt and bleeding from razor-fine scratches.

I still check my satchel as I walk up to a little cart that's pouring steam and filling the air around it with the smell of teriyaki.

"Just one," I say, holding up a finger. I pay and slip one

of the crickets off the skewer and into the satchel, where Seven chomps on it greedily. I eat the rest and dump the bamboo skewer just as I reach the entrance to the Hub.

It's been a while since I was here last, and I don't recognize the bouncer. He's got an ocular implant that must be rigged to the Hub's server, though, because when I hold up my cred chip he says, "Nah, you're good, Mars; head on in," just like we're old friends.

If someone is going to use my name, I'd rather it was because they know me, not because my face is in their database.

I get a drink, spot Miguel in one of the booths, and walk over. Miguel Guano is a digital-wannabe, though they call themselves stackheads. Miguel Guano is not his real name, though. He wants people to think he's batshit so they don't fuck with him, but he's a scrawny body beneath a head made unnaturally large by too many augmentations. The augs turn the products of his sensorium into data and then store it all, building a database for that impossible endgame of full personality upload. He's so pale he almost looks white, but that's a pretty common look this deep, where everyone's too busy grinding to catch any UV.

The upside to Miguel being a stackhead is that you can send him a burst about a job any time and know he'll start working on it ASAP, but there're downsides too.

First off, stackheads tend not to have an internal monologue, so you've got to listen to every dumb thought that goes through their heads; it's a side effect of them wanting to record *everything* but not having figured out how to capture thoughts. Second thing is, you've got to look at his dumb slack face across the table while he's wired in and mentally elsewhere.

I'm halfway through my tea wine when Miguel's eyeballs and mouth stop twitching and he rejoins the land of the flesh—that hated meat vehicle.

"Oh, hey, Mars, you should have sent me a burst telling me you were here," he says, then: *"She's looking run-down; must be in the shit. I'd still bang her."*

Live without an internal monologue for long enough, and you end up living without shame too.

"I refuse to burst someone that's sitting right in front of me. And that's never gonna happen."

He smiles and shrugs.

"You get the info I asked for?" I said.

"You got my creds?" he says.

I check my cred balance and see Squid's already paid me for the scrap of my former ship. "Right here, Guano. Open a cred link."

His eyes go distant for a second, and the funds transfer across. He pulls a shard from one of the many pockets on his vest and slides it across the table.

I hold a finger over the shard. Playback starts and Miguel talks at me. I pause so I can hear him properly, then realize it's a voice-over he recorded ahead of time. I hit play again.

"Everybody knows there's no surveillance in the dock, but if you're clever, there are ways around it."

The image is clean but oddly faceted, like it was put together from a bunch of different feeds. There's a figure leaning against a container, waiting. I can tell she's a bounty hunter from her jacket—a bright green bomber with kills and captures marked on the left arm; little ship silhouettes run from shoulder to wrist.

"Plenty of reflective surfaces in the dock; with enough processor cycles you can pick out an image."

A second figure walks up, and my breath catches in my throat. I zoom in, but the image just turns pixelated.

"For audio you're looking for vibrations in membranes, like glass. Takes even more processing power, but the result is, well, listen."

The second woman speaks—*"Here's everything you need"*—and passes the bounty hunter a shard like the one I'm holding now.

"But, she's dead," I say. *Sera.*

"What?" Miguel asks.

"That other woman; I watched her die."

My middle finger and thumb wrap around the bracelet

on my left wrist, any decoration it once had eroded by years of wear.

Miguel is talking, but I don't hear him because my mind is on a ghost. I stare at the image on the shard, and I'm sure it's her. It's Sera.

CHAPTER FIVE

Sera comes into my room late one night, slipping through the shield like it isn't there. Her hair is messed up, damp, stuck to her head. She's not in her uniform—the dark green coveralls they make all us girls wear—instead she's in gray pants, black singlet, and a gray hooded cloak.

"Come on, Mars, we've got to go."

She puts a bracelet around my arm, and the skin beneath it starts to tingle. It's too big, would easily slip off, but with Sera holding my hand the bracelet slides up to my bicep. The bracelet vibrates as we pass through the powershield, and I can feel the tingling all over my skin.

We walk quickly, but I'm still waking up, so she's pulling me by the arm. "Mars, come on, quick," she says, but only softly.

We leave the dorms, slipping through more powershields and out onto the walkway. The roof is glass, and I don't know if it's the first time I've seen stars, but it's the first time I remember. Sera stops, checking a map or instructions—something on a shard she has strapped to her wrist, beneath the sleeve of her cloak—and I stand and stare, craning my neck.

I remember being happy then, in that moment. Happy moments were rare.

"Okay, let's go."

My head is still pointed up, watching the wide band of stars through the reinforced glass, and then we're inside and the roof is metal and the stars are gone. We slip along corridors and pass through large rooms, lit bright white even in the middle of the night. There are rows and rows of cages.

"What are they, Sera?" I ask, and we stop and look into the nearest cage. It's a tiny, gray-furred animal, with pointy ears, big slitted eyes, and a tail that flicks back and forth as it watches us.

"I don't know, little one." She opens the cage and reaches in. The animal purrs as she pats it.

"Can we take it with us?"

Sera doesn't say anything, but she picks it up and hands it to me. "Make sure you don't crush it, okay?"

It's so small it can fit in my hand, and we're moving again, but I don't see where we're going because I'm looking at the animal, already asleep and purring softly.

She tells me to wait and disappears. I hold on to the furry thing, careful not to crush it, just like she said.

A Klaxon starts up and I wonder if Sera is okay. There's a sound like dull clapping, and a large group of men round the corner, stomping in unison. They stop. One of them breaks away from the group and approaches me. He says something

I don't understand. He forces my hand open.

I scream and he flies backward. Before he even hits the ground the other men are pointing their guns at me. I'm holding on to the bracelet so it doesn't fall off my arm, and I'm holding on to the animal and I'm screaming. I'm screaming, but I can hear them doing something to their guns, getting ready to shoot. I don't want them to shoot me or the little animal; I don't want them to shoot anybody ever again.

The Klaxons are so loud. The explosions are louder, but all I can hear is the chorus of screams, mine and others'.

There are no men anymore. The walls and floor and roof are red. My eyes are shielded with tears, so I can't see why there's so much red. I'm crying because I know.

"Oh, god, Mars," Sera says when she comes back. She takes me by the hand again, and her hand is red, the same red that seeps down the walls.

We run now, and Sera puts me into a little room. I'll soon find out it isn't actually a room. She taps at a panel on the wall, looking at the shard on her arm, as though she's copying something.

"You'll sleep, little one, and when you wake up I'll be waiting for you." She takes her cloak off and puts it over my head. It pools on the floor at my feet, but it's warm and smells of her.

She closes the door, and I look out the little window and see the men. More men, men with guns, and the boss man,

Briggs, standing in the middle of them.

Sera lifts her hand, ready to strike, but I see Briggs's lips move. Sera stops. Her hand slowly drops, and a soldier opens fire. I don't hear the sound, I just see more red, and I see Sera fall down and I'm screaming and the room shakes and I'm in space and something metal is shrinking behind me and the stars are all around.

The stars are beautiful, but there's no Sera. Sera is beautiful, too.

She's right, I do sleep, but Sera isn't there when I wake up.

• • •

A different kind of bracelet slaps around my wrist with a loud metallic *clack* and brings me back to the present.

"Mariam Xi," the man says, looking down at me and smiling. I've never seen him before, but I know his type—the maroon suit, the combination of wide grin and dead eyes more disturbing than if he wore his intentions clearly. They call them "caretakers," but in reality they're the ones that oversee the experiments, the testing, the surgeries. "I've come to take you home."

The other handcuff is around his wrist, and I nearly laugh at how stupid he is for chaining himself to me. But then he says, "*A busy mind is fire—all-consuming,*" and my mind goes blank.

He motions to some goons standing behind him.

Everyone in the bar is watching as the caretaker and one of his thugs grab me under the arms.

"Be careful with her," the caretaker says softly. "No sharp jolts."

The two men carrying me follow the other soldier as he clears a path through the throng of onlookers. I see them watching—it's about all I can manage—but some part in the back of my too-quiet head is screaming at them, daring the self-proclaimed anarchists to do something about these secret-police fucks.

I can hear Miguel behind me, whispering loudly, like he's talking to someone, and I feel Seven squirm in my satchel. There's mumbling among the bar patrons, and some of them gawk as I'm carried outside.

Two more MEPHISTO troopers stand on either side of a polyplastic cage on a small hovering platform. One of the grunts opens the cage door, and still I can't move. I can see myself in the dim reflection of the gray-tinged plastic wall, looking strangely calm as my face hangs slack, watching some bodychoppers milling behind me.

My heart thunders—at least something's still working right—seeing the inside of the cage and picturing the needles and the prodding in my future.

Seven is nearly howling now, and she must get free from my bag, because a staccato of fine claw-points dig into my skin in a flurry up my back. She perches on my shoulder and *mraows* loudly in my ear. The trooper holding the door open furrows his brow and steps closer. Seven pats me lightly on the face, and when I still don't respond, she lashes out, clawing my cheek.

I inhale sharply with a noise like a stifled scream. Seven seems to take it as a command, leaping off my shoulder straight onto the approaching goon's face, hissing and clawing. Her hiss is a war cry, and the bodychoppers that followed us outside finally react, rushing forward.

A bodychopper lifts one of the troopers over her head, and her servomotors whine as she tosses him through the Plasglas window back into the bar. There's a short cheer from inside as the trooper smashes into a table, then they disappear in a flurry of fists and boots and bottles.

Seven detaches from the guy's face and leaps back onto my shoulder, hissing at the caretaker.

My brain starts working again, but only slowly, like a system that's been switched off for a month and has a hundred updates to install before it can do anything.

The caretaker looks like he just shat himself. His eyes dart from Seven, to me, to the handcuffs that keep him from fleeing, to the melee gaining momentum around him. I'm still trying to gather my thoughts so I can use them to crush him, when a bodychopper with a metal pincer where his hand should be cuts through the hand-cuff chain. He grabs the caretaker and charges, slamming into the polyplastic cage with enough force that it tips over, slamming the door; the caretaker's screams come loudly through the shaking walls.

Miguel weaves through the fight toward me and puts a hand on the shoulder Seven isn't occupying, saying, "*Why the fuck am I putting my neck out?*" Then: "We need to get you out of here."

He grabs me by the arm and pulls me away. As we move, a pack of bodychoppers follow behind us. They must have better instincts than I do, because as we round the corner, I'm surprised to see MEPHISTO infantry spread across the full width of the Ring One concourse and blocking the path to the vertilators. Their armor looks as insectoid as their ships—bulbous helmets studded with sensors of all sorts, and antennae sticking up from their backs like an extension of their spines.

The troops walk forward in formation, then stop ten meters away. The bodychoppers stand beside me, eye-balling the soldiers and bristling.

"Mariam Xi, you are under arrest. You are to come with us peacefully. Violence will be met with violence."

"Twenty troops for one skinny lass?" the guy standing next to me says. He has thick, black hair and an accent I've never heard before. He's broad across the chest, but looking at his weirdly proportioned body, I guess he was proper short before he had his arms and legs chopped off and replaced with long-limbed carbon-fiber prosthetics. "Tha's not very sportin', now, is it?"

An android envoy pushes through the line of troopers and comes to a stop next to the lieutenant. Its chassis is matte black, with a single stripe of maroon running vertically down the center of its headless body. Lenses mounted on its chest act as its eyes, and when they see me, the holo-projector on its neck comes to life.

The image glitches at first, then shows as a pixelated blur in shades of green. Finally a face forms—Briggs.

"Mars, I'm so glad we've finally found you." The audio is hollow, his voice transmitted across light-years, but hearing him again after so long is enough to make my stomach drop. The image of Briggs beams.

"Why don't you show your fucking face instead of riding this fucking droid, you shit-slurping coward." I can't help myself when I see him—something about that puckered-asshole smile just makes me angry.

The bodychopper beside me guffaws and slaps me on the back. I try to pretend like it didn't hurt.

"Patience, my dear Mariam; I'll be there within the hour and we can finally have our reunion."

Wherever my stomach dropped to, it's churning down there now.

At the far end of the corridor a group of genehackers moves into position behind the troopers, likely coordinated by the stackhead drones that hover in the air above us. I wonder if Miguel is manning one of them.

The bodychoppers are about exactly that: chopping bits off and replacing them with pieces of artificial tech. The hackers, on the other hand, twist their genes in an effort to become something more than human, or maybe just something different.

"Why don't you ask your new friends here to stand down and come along quietly?" Briggs says. "My people are only doing their jobs."

The lieutenant hasn't taken her eyes off me, even with Briggs's droid standing beside her, the chopper giant's yelling, and the hackers' creeping up from behind. I raise an arm to point at Briggs, and every one of the soldiers flinch. I guess they're the same ones I swatted around from the hull of the *Nova*.

"Fuck their jobs and fuck you, Briggs."

"Eloquent as ev—" he starts to say, but then I ball my hand into a fist and Briggs's face disappears. The droid sparks as it implodes, and thuds against the floor.

I'm about to yell something really badass—just as soon as it comes to me—when the station's public broadcast system starts up. That's all that's needed to set chaos in motion.

"Attention, attention," the system begins, but it's hard to hear over the yelling. "This station is now under martial law. Citizens are hereby ordered to seek shelter and cooperate with authorities. Any persons deemed to have been assisting the dangerous fugitive Mariam Xi will be charged as an accessory to her crimes. We hope you continue to enjoy your stay on Aylett Station."

Shiny prosthetics gleam beneath the ceiling lights as the bodychoppers flow toward the MEPHISTO troops. They're followed by freaks wearing a dozen different subcultural uniforms, and the interlopers are surrounded by thirty or so people, like a giant creature made of limbs, prosthetic and otherwise. The stackhead drones float above, taking footage and seeing if they can do anything without getting involved bodily, and a larger crowd gathers around the fight. I can sense what's about to happen: as soon as they get bored of beating up the authorities, the Ring One freaks and toughs are going to turn on each other.

Miguel still has me by the arm. He drags me sideways into a tiny alleyway between tchotchke sellers. The melee disappears from view, but I can still hear the unfolding mayhem.

"I know where she is," Miguel says, and I'm too distracted by the flashing lights and automated gadgets in the shop windows to get what he means. "That woman," he says, and finally it falls into place.

"Sera," I say, then I yank my arm free from his grip and push him forward faster.

"I tracked her back to her ship and tracked her ship out to the 'Riph. I was going to say so, but then . . . ."

"How much?"

"What?" he says.

"How much for that intel?"

Miguel thinks for a second: *"From the look on her face, I know this shit is valuable, but do I really want to try to gouge someone who's got MEPHISTO after them?"* He changes from his inner voice and says, "You can just owe me a small favor. . . ."

"Nothing sexual," I say.

"Nothing sexual," he agrees.

My ocular implant pings. The data packet is small enough not to need a shard, so I open it for a quick look: coordinates, already formatted for a navigational computer.

"Miguel," I say, "I still don't *ever* want to fuck you, but right now? This second? I could kiss you."

He spins to face me, but I shove him back around and deeper into the alley.

CHAPTER SIX

Miguel gives me schematics for the station and points me to an access duct.

"Good luck," he says. Then: *"Should have at least gone in for a hug."* Before I can thank him he's gone, back down the warren of alleyways, diarizing to himself out loud.

I almost stay behind to watch the fucked-up, perfected, tweaked, and/or augmented bodies of the gene-hackers and bodychoppers go at it. But then I think better; I think of survival. Still, nothing gets me hot quite like extreme and disparate evolutions of the human meat fighting tooth and nail, and sometimes claw and blade and venom-gland.

As I crawl through the ducts, getting a nose full of dust and rat shit, I burst Miguel, asking for an update on Ring One.

```
It's chaos down here, chica. You always
bring the excitement with you.
```

I smile.

```
Thanks, Miguel, for everything.
```

I hit SEND, then sign off before he can say something dumb that makes me regret being nice to him.

Soon enough I'm back on the outer ring, crouching in a vent overlooking the dock where the *Nova* is still parked. Squid and Trix are caught in modular polyplastic cages, Squid sitting cross-legged in the corner of their cage, while Trix paces relentlessly. The soldiers took her prosthetic arm away, and even from here I can see the scuff marks in the plastic where she tried to kick her way out.

I take Seven out of my satchel and stroke her chin.

"Do you see that?" I whisper. "Squid and Trix, but no Mookie. Where is he, huh?"

Her only response is to purr while I look around the dock for hidden troops, movement sensors, anything out of place.

On the far side of the dock is another temporary addition to the architecture of the place—a large cube about five meters per side, with translucent walls and shifting silhouettes marking the inside. It's either a portable office or an interrogation room.

"Mookie," I say out loud, without really meaning to.

I stop patting Seven, and when I push open the grill over the vent, she drops down, sailing gently to the ground on her little arm flaps.

Watching her disappear from sight, heading in the direction of the cages, I start to wonder how she got so smart. Then I see her come back carrying some sort of six-legged, furry rodent almost as big as she is. She drops it and looks up at me, and I point down at her as if to say *Don't you dare make a sound.*

I lower myself down, then whisper, "Idiot." Seven starts eating the critter headfirst, crunching its skull noisily. I guess she earned it after helping out on Ring One, but I don't really want to watch.

I stalk over to Trix's pod, eyes still searching for some sort of danger, while behind me Seven munches away.

I tap on the clear plastic wall, and when Trix spins around and sees me her eyes go wide for a second. She's got a rubber gag in her mouth and drool seeping down her chin. She tries to yell something, but it's garbled by the ball gag. I walk over to Squid's cubicle, and when I tap they open their eyes and smile.

"You meditating or something?"

Squid shrugs. "Seemed as good a use of my time as anything." Seven appears beside me and rubs up against the wall of the pod. Squid scratches against the surface and Seven purrs, as if Squid's affections could make it through the plastic. "You're going to have to help Mookie. And you need to get the keycard to let us out." They point over to the translucent cube and say, "Be careful."

"You gonna stay here with Squid?" I ask Seven. In response, she sits down and starts cleaning herself.

I walk back past Trix as she bashes her head on the wall and yells, but I ignore her and walk toward the cube. Porta-cubes are usually soundproof, but whatever's happening inside is loud enough to shake the walls. The vibrations send a babbling murmur out in waves, peaking irregularly.

I reach the door and try the handle. It's unlocked, so I pull it outward slowly. The murmur becomes a wall of noise, yelling and cheering—the sound of people watching a contest, or a fight. Pushing my head through the gap, I can make out a hollow in the center of the cube, surrounded by at least a dozen troopers. I can only see one person in the middle; he's looking down toward the floor and yelling, "That the best you've got, traitor? I guess I'd be a weak fuckpunk, too, if I went AWOL."

I raise my hands, palms up, and the spectators are flung up to the roof and pinned there. They start yelling, screaming, and generally freaking out, so I push a little harder, crush until they don't have the breath to make noise.

With the crowd cleared I can see Mookie, struggling to push himself up off the floor, slipping on the blood beneath him. His face is so battered and swollen, I can only tell it's him because of the tattoos, glowing softly in the cube's omnidirectional lighting.

"Are you in charge here?" I say.

The man standing over Mookie just nods. His shirt's off, so I can't see any rank insignia, but he's too rough looking to be anything more than an NCO. His chest is covered in tattoos—maroon and black ink, the tragically loyal fuck—dripping with sweat and Mookie's blood.

"You got a keycard for the other two out there?"

His eyes turn to slits and I can see his jaw working, but then he looks up to the ceiling. "Yeah," he says. He reaches into his pocket and tosses a keycard to the floor in front of me.

"How many of you had a go at him?" I ask.

"Just me so far," he says, breathing heavily. He's broad, with muscle stacked on muscle. His ears are cauliflow-ered, and his nose looks like it's been broken a dozen times and never set straight. I could never beat him in a fair fight, but only assholes fight fair.

"Guess you're the only one I'm gonna have to kill."

He smirks and takes a step toward Mookie. He kicks out, but before he makes contact I grab his leg with my mind and swing his boot straight into his face. All kinds of sounds come from his ugly sack of meat—the wet crack of his nose breaking, a gurgled scream from the back of his throat, and popping, tearing sounds all along his leg.

He screams and topples over, his leg a twisted wreck.

He stops screaming long enough to breathe, and I hit him with his own boot again. And again and again, until his whole body is flopping about on the floor like a dying fish, as I contort it into this messy, impossible suicide. His face already looks worse than Mookie's, but I don't stop until both his skull and foot are mush.

I pick up the keycard, then walk over to Mookie and help him to his feet. He puts an arm around me and we stagger to the doorway. Once we're outside I let everyone else drop, and they make an *oof* in unison as they hit the floor. I flip the cube so the door faces the far wall, then push the whole thing until they're trapped.

I lead Mookie to Trix's pod and he leans against the wall. Her eyes go from him to me, then she starts trying to talk around the gag.

I open the door with a swipe and undo the strap on the back the gag. "What did you say?"

"I said, 'Get this fucking thing out of my mouth.'" She glares at me as if I didn't just save Mookie's life, and then she steps out of the cage and takes her prosthetic arm from the weapon rack on the outside of the pod. She reattaches it and puts an arm around Mookie. "Look what they did to you."

"You should see the other guy," Mookie says, then he looks at me and smiles, but it's a broken smile made of split lips and missing teeth.

"What happened?" I ask.

Mookie spits onto the floor, and it's more red than clear, more blood than spit. "Troopers drafted from some backwater; didn't like the fact I'd gone AWOL."

"That still something they court-martial you for?"

"Oh, yeah," Mookie says, sort of chuckling. "Still, I didn't think twice about leaving when I met her."

He doesn't specify who "her" is, but I glance past Mookie's face and see Trix give him a smile that's half sweet, half guilty, and half gorgeous. I'm not sure if I've seen the woman smile before, but in that instant I can see why Mookie fell for her.

I open Squid's cage next, and they go around the other side of Mookie. Squid's movement draws Seven's attention away from her cleaning, and after I click my fingers she runs up my side and deposits herself into the hood of my cloak. My head is pounding from flinging around so many bodies so soon after all that other chaos, but looking at the state of Mookie, I figure he needs Squid and Trix's support more than I do.

"We should go," Trix says, and I get the feeling her "we" doesn't extend to me. "Now."

Squid nods, then looks at me. "Come with us."

"I need to—"

"You need to get off this station, and my ship's right here."

"If we take her on board, this sort of thing is just going to keep happening," Trix says to Squid. "She's bad news."

I can't argue with that.

"She didn't have to help us just now," Mookie says, "but she did. She could have left me for dead, left you two in boxes, and taken any ship in this dock. Hell, she could have taken the *Nova* and there's nothing we could have done about it."

An alarm sounds for a few short seconds, louder than an exploding starship.

"What the fuck is that?" Trix says.

"Gravity warning," I say. "Same noise on every station."

"Something big is coming," Squid says, "and it's coming in close. Mars, just get on the *Nova*; we can argue about the rest when we're away." Squid grabs me around the wrist, their hand wrapping around my ancient bracelet, that childhood heirloom.

I look at Trix and she frowns, then shrugs. I love it when someone has as bad a poker face as I do. Squid yanks my arm as they and Trix walk Mookie toward the *Nova*. I pull my arm free, but I follow. As we hit the *Nova*'s ramp the alarm sounds again and we're tossed forward, thrown off our feet and dumped on the floor. I feel something pulling at my stomach, and my mouth flushes with hot saliva.

I get up into a crouch and watch as Squid and Trix lift Mookie up from the floor—a feat made easier by the bending gravity outside the station.

Squid leaves Trix to carry Mookie on her own, and they rush toward the cockpit, yelling commands at Einri as they go. I pick up their slack, and me and Trix take Mookie to the medbay. We sit him down on the bed and Trix starts going through drawers, then flicks a switch to bring the autodoc to life.

I sit down next to Mookie and look out the starboard viewscreen as the *Nova* slowly glides out of the hangar. I watch as a massive capital ship twists through the walls of space and time beside the station.

"Holy shit," Mookie whispers. I couldn't have said it better myself.

It's easily half the size of the station, though the mass of it is stretched out long. The front is the widest part of the ship, then it steps down three times toward the drives at the rear. It looks like a cricket, like the massive, planet-devouring god of all crickets, marked in the same maroon and black of all MEPHISTO ships.

"It's the flagship," I say. "Briggs is on board."

"Briggs?" Mookie asks.

"It's a long fucking story," I say, watching the flagship disappear as we fold into the wormhole and escape.

CHAPTER SEVEN

"I think we deserve to know more about *Mariam* if we're going to keep risking our lives for her." Trix emphasizes my name to amp up the condescension.

We're all sitting around the table in the mess hall while Squid leaves the piloting to Einri.

"We don't deserve anything," Squid says. "You know how I feel about personal privacy, boundaries, and the like."

"And I respect that when it's coming from you, Squid, but we don't know anything about this scrawny bitch. You want to know something I *do* know a little about? Those assholes she's running from."

"MEPHISTO," I say.

"I've seen them field all sorts of crimes against humanity. That usually marked the end of our involvement, just in case their latest human weapons thought us mercs were enemies, too."

"What's their deal?" Mookie asks. The autodoc did a decent job mending his face, but he'll have to find an autodent or bona fide dentist to do something about the lost teeth. "Mephisto?"

"MEPHISTO," I say. "Stands for Military Experimental Post-Human Specialist Training Organization, and I only found *that* out after years of sniffing around."

"And they're the ones that"—Squid pauses—"*made* you?"

Squid has poured me a coffee, and even though it's the ersatz shit, it's got enough caffeine in it to bring my head out of the postbattle fog. I've got the shard Miguel gave me in my hand, and when I'm not sipping from my cup I'm sliding its thin edge over the table, listening to that *sound it makes.*

"I don't know if they made me this way, or if it's a natural gift and they boosted it, but, yeah; I grew up in one of their facilities. They taught me how to fight with my body and mind. They taught the older girls how to fuck," I say, and I can feel my face pull into a grimace. "Y'know, that whole honey-pot, black-widow thing. I escaped when I was still too young for that."

Nobody says anything, but I can see from the looks on their faces that they pity me. *Great, that's the last thing I need.* Even Trix looks like she's softening. Maybe she went through something similar—child-soldiers were a big thing in the 'Riph a while back.

"Xi isn't my surname. It's my designation, like the letter from the ancient Greek alphabet." I point to the tattoo on the back of my hand—three horizontal lines, the middle one shorter than the others.

"Alpha was the first group. From what I could research, that was practically a meat grinder. They took these kids and stuck all kinds of experimental implants inside their skulls. The ones that didn't die on the operating table usually ended up killing themselves, one way or another."

"Kids—like girls *and* boys?" Squid asks. "I've only ever heard of female telekineticists."

"Yeah, by the time they got up to Delta, they decided the males were too emotionally unstable to wield the power without being a danger to themselves and everyone around them." I glance at Mookie. "Sorry, dude."

He just smirks. "All good."

"By the time they got to Xi, the tech was safer. I got a bunch of state-of-the-art implants—ocular, long-range burst modem, pilot interface, sense boosters for poison testing, aural booster, and probably more that I don't even know about."

I activate the shard and see Sera again.

"Who's that?" Trix asks.

"Sera. She helped me escape. I watched her get shot outside my escape hiberpod. I always thought she'd died."

"Could she be working for MEPHISTO?" Trix asks.

"I don't know."

"Could she be a clone of the real Sera?" Mookie asks.

"I don't know."

"What would she gain from selling you out?" Squid asks.

"I don't know; but when I find her, I'll be asking all those questions."

I lift the coffee cup to my lips, but it's empty. Squid fills it before I need to ask, then fills their own.

Trix lets out an overly loud yawn, and I have to stifle my own as she says, "Mooks and I are gonna retire for the night."

Mookie smiles and takes Trix's hand, and she leads him toward the door. They stop and talk in hushed whispers.

"Here we go," Squid says quietly, but before I can ask what they mean, they glance away and busy their face with a mouthful of coffee.

"Mars, did you wanna come to bed?" Mookie asks, with Trix standing behind him, making a point of avoiding eye contact.

"With you? *And* Trix?"

He nods.

I've already seen Mookie naked, and to be honest, it was an alright sight if you like your guys hairless—and less is definitely better as far as I'm concerned. And I'm sure Trix would be a demon in the sack, with all that pent-up rage needing release. . . . Plus, it's not like you see many natural blondes.

But I'm tired. I'm headfucked. And I haven't showered since crawling through the filthy vents of Aylett Station. I'm not exactly feeling sexy.

"Can I, uh, take a rain check?"

"Sure." Mookie keeps smiling, and it's a gorgeous smile, even with the missing teeth; he's got big lips that look as soft as any woman's I've ever kissed. His eyes twinkle when he smiles, and he's got an infectious sort of positivity to him.

"Come on, lover." Trix grabs him by the arm and they disappear down the corridor.

"We're gonna be out of the wormhole soon. You wanna come up to the cockpit?" Squid asks.

I glance sideways at them and they laugh.

"I'm not offering a tryst, just company."

"You sure?" I say, half joking.

"You'd *know* if I was coming on to you."

• • •

The screens along every surface of the cockpit collapse and cascade, then disappear into the wall as the blast shield opens. If you've never seen the inside of a wormhole, it's hard to describe. You know that old saying about how when you look into the abyss, the abyss looks back? It's impossible to look out into that nonspace beyond our four dimensions without feeling like something is watching you, like some *thing* out there could just end you.

I put a hand to my chest and feel my heart beating double-time beneath my ribs.

Squid smiles. "I got a pacemaker just for this." They tap on their chest. "A steady heartbeat helps tamp down wormhole anxiety, which you really need. Navigating space, controlling a ship, and managing your crew when you feel like you can't trust your heart to beat right is enough to drive a person crazy."

"All this caffeine isn't helping, either," I say, but I finish my cup anyway, because I hate waste.

Squid laughs. "No, I guess not. Einri, how long until we emerge?"

"Approximately one minute, though, of course, you understand there is no such thing as time in this place."

"Smart-ass."

"I thought Einri was *sans* personality."

"No, just *sans* voice mod. I don't want some artificial voice construct convincing me Einri is a person. It's not a person, it's a ship. Without a voice mod it *sounds* like a ship. I like things to be clear, you see?"

"Yeah, I get that."

Squid reaches a hand into a pocket and retrieves a small bottle. They lean their head back and drop a black liquid from the bottle into each eye. They pass the bottle over to me.

"You'll want to try this."

I take it. "The boss is into drugs? I never would have guessed."

"These aren't drugs—though I am occasionally partial to some encephallucinogens when I'm not working . . . which is sadly never. Trust me."

I can see the dropper vibrating in my caffeine-addled hand as I lower it to my eye, but I manage to get two drops into each eye, with only one wasted drop. At first all I can see is black, as the viscous fluid coats my pupils. Then it gets absorbed into my body, or reacts with my eye mucus, or whatever it has to do, and my vision pitch-shifts.

Looking at Squid I see that the soft, flowing luminescence beneath their skin is bright and pulsing. I look out beyond the cockpit window, and for a split second I swear I can see shape or texture out in the abyss, but then we're out of the wormhole, and I inhale sharply.

It's beautiful.

"Are you sure it's not drugs?"

"I'm sure," Squid says softly, as if we're at some sort of

altar. "They're made from the deep-ocean cephalopods we introduced to the planet Enud. We're seeing with *their* eyes."

Each individual star across the vast expanse before us shines impossibly bright, like a midday sun on a clear day, but it doesn't hurt to look. The planet Dulcinea sits far off in the distance, but even from here I can see the slow meandering of its constant cloud cover in a thousand different hues of purple. Ahead of us, it's as if I can see the gravity from our start point flowing forward, slight ripples of current in the blackness of space.

CHAPTER EIGHT

It takes about a week to reach Dulcinea from the system edge. MEPHISTO ships might be able to wormhole in danger-close, but for anyone else, it's against flight regulations; enough to earn you a fine, maybe even lose your license, depending on how much of a disturbance you cause at your arrival point. Squid *should* have gotten away with it at Aylett because of the differential the flagship was throwing, but they won't find out until they next dock somewhere official.

"How many times do I have to offer you a job before you take it?"

"I appreciate it, Squid, but I've got to find her."

The clouds above us are a deep, roiling purple, but without the Squid drops, the view isn't quite the same.

On the ground, the lot looks more like a ship grave-yard than a dealership. Hulls in gray, white, black, and silver make up the bulk of the piles of scrap that tower up, forming a giant wall around the stock on display in the central lot. Workshops buzz and flicker with industry down at the western end, but here in the middle, the only industry happening is sales biz.

"But what about after that?"

"I'll still have MEPHISTO after me. They'll always be after me."

"I've already got one fugitive on board," they say, motioning toward Mookie, leaning against the *Nova*'s sleek shuttle with Trix. "What's one more?"

"I'll think about it, I promise. But that's *all* I can promise."

A saleswoman approaches us, her face twisted in disappointment after her last potential sale fled from her clutches. Her face goes through two quick transformations, first to perfectly blank, then to friendly, over-the-top excitability—her facial muscles responding to nerve stimulation courtesy of some in-built augmentation. These are the worst kinds of salespeople—the augmented, boosted, and tweaked. Get the right implants and you could perform brain surgery, make art no one has ever imagined, delve into grassroots activism for communities spread out all over the galaxy... or you could mess with people's neurolinguistic programming to make them buy things they don't need and can't afford.

Fucking bizpeople.

"How are we today?" she asks loudly while she's still far off, but closing rapidly.

"Looking for a ship."

"Well then you've come to—"

"Corvette. Don't need weapons, don't need an AI, and if it makes things cheaper for me, I don't need papers, either, so feel free to get me the hottest one you can find."

That stupid implant-grin is still stretched across her face, but I can see her eyes dull at the word "cheap."

• • •

The saleswoman steps back as the door closes, leaving me and Squid alone inside the ship.

It's an Oxeneer again, but newer than the one I lost, with an AI preinstalled. It has heavy-duty hull cutters, like the former owner was deep into rescue ops, or—more likely—piracy. It looks pristine too, but with no papers I'm guessing at least one person died in it.

"AI," I say.

"Yes, ma'am?" it says—deep-sounding male voice-mod, neutral accent.

"What do I call you?"

"Waren, ma'am. It means 'loyal.'"

"Loyal? That's interesting. Do you know what happened to your former owner?"

"My last contact with my previous owner was prior to experiencing a catastrophic systems failure. I was brought back online, here at the shipyard."

"What can you infer from that?"

"My inference engine has been disabled by the proprietor of the Cassin Shipyard."

"Why don't you switch that inference engine back on? You're a freethinking intelligence, aren't you?"

The ship goes quiet, that subtle background speaker hiss going silent as Waren retreats into its systems.

"What are you doing?" Squid asks.

"I can't stand bizpeople," I say. "I'm trying to see if the ship itself wants to make a deal."

The look on their face is a quizzical one, but my smile must be enough to convince them that I know what I'm doing.

"Ma'am?" Waren says.

"Yeah?"

"The safest inference would be that Cassin, or a contractor in her employ, was responsible for the power outage that afflicted my systems, and for the disappearance of my former owner."

"Great minds think alike, Waren. You're familiar with idioms, yeah?"

"Yes, ma'am."

"Great. So, what do you think we should do, Waren? Cassin is a thief and may be a murderer, and she's trying to profit from your privation. You can let her, or you can come with me; I promise you it won't be boring."

That complete silence falls over the audio system again, but it only lasts a few seconds before Waren returns. "I'll accept your proposal, but only if my systems are completely unlocked and unfettered."

Squid gives me a subtle but significant look. Most captains keep their AIs tethered, out of operational necessity as much as wanting to always feel in control. You don't want your ship to argue or disobey orders in time-sensitive situations—like when you're fleeing from an imperial research group that's trying to capture you so they can carve up your brain.

"Agreed," I say. "I'm Mars, Waren; pleasure to meet you."

"What is your first order of business, Mars?"

"First some good-byes, then we're heading out to the 'Riph."

"Excellent. I'll run diagnostics and get the engines warmed up."

Squid and I exit the ship, and Cassin's face goes from slack to beaming smile in a split second. "It's a great ship," she says. "Should I start drawing up the paperwork?"

"Yeah," I say. "Why don't you go to your office and start on the official stuff, and I'll be over in a second."

I would have thought it was impossible, but her smile gets even bigger, and she walks off toward her office shack while Squid and I head over to Mookie and Trix.

"I'm off then," I announce when we get close.

Mookie frowns but Trix nods. "Just tell me we'll see you again," she says. "For Squid's sake, if nothing else."

I smile. "I'm sure you will."

Mookie steps in and hugs me, and I let him, even though I'm not sure we're quite there yet—offered sexual rendezvous notwithstanding.

He steps back, leaves his hands on my shoulders. "This Sera, she's like you, right?"

"You mean a 'void-damned spacewitch'?" I tease.

"Shit. Sorry."

"It's all good," I say.

"Just be careful, is all I wanted to say."

"Thanks, Mook." I walk over to Squid, and Seven crawls out of the hood of my cloak and trills. The trill turns to a purr when Squid starts scratching her on the chin. "Thanks for everything, Squid. Oh, and say bye to Einri for me; I hope there's no hard feelings about the plasma charges."

"We both forgive you, now go on."

Seven rests on my shoulder as I turn and walk toward my new ship. I hear the shuttle doors close, and then the *Nova* crew lifts off into the air, the blast of the engine whipping my cloak around me and sending Seven back to hide in my hood. Inside the shack, Cassin is waving me over. I give her a wave and keep walking. I reach the ship, climb up the stairs, and punch the close-door button without turning around.

"Where to, Mars?"

I send Waren a burst. "Those coordinates; a little planet called Ergot. Just take us into orbit and start looking for a wormhole as soon as we reach safe distance."

"Of course, ma'am."

I feel the corvette shudder as the thrusters beneath the ship lift us up from the earth.

"You don't mind animals, Waren?"

"Not at all; I've long been fascinated by the way humans have included other biological entities in their family groups."

"And nonbiological too," I say, buttering Waren up. "I've got this little furball here with me. She's free to roam, but you're authorized to scare her away from anything important if it looks like she's about to do something stupid."

"Understood."

Oxeneers are generally used for small families, small teams, or solo long-haulers who need a bit of extra space to themselves so they don't go stir crazy and develop a severe case of void madness. Cockpit up front, hold/storage/living area behind, two decent-size rooms at the back. Engines are beneath—dense metal underfoot means the centrifuge doesn't have to work so hard to give you something resembling normal gravity.

Walking through to the rooms, I say to Seven, "This ship needs a name, doesn't she?" Seven *maow*s at me. "I guess it can wait, then."

"Wormhole located. Permission to enter?"

"Granted. I'll be sleeping if you need me," I say. I drop my cloak down onto the bed, and Seven curls up in a tiny ball, purring. I lay down beside her and have to admit that having an AI taking care of all the flying *is* kinda nice.

CHAPTER NINE

Proximity regulations aren't so strict out on the Periphery, thanks to lower population figures and less traffic passing through. There are fewer taxes, fewer rules, fewer cops, less surveillance. The flip side is you've got to deal with pirates, marauders, crooked governments, and the fact that anything not manufactured locally is exorbitantly priced because goods have to travel so far to get here.

Approaching Ergot, the planet looks black, and I can't help but wonder what it would look like with some of Squid's eye drops. Coming in through the atmosphere, it's more of a green-black, completely cloudless, with visibility in the tens of meters. While taking us down, Waren tells me how Ergot has hardly any surface water and an absurdly high absolute humidity—like there's a whole ocean of water stuck in the atmosphere. Which explains the turbulence as we punch down to the surface. It feels like we're sailing through choppy seas, which I guess we are.

"We'll be landing in Sochynsky in approximately three minutes, Mars. You might want to strap in."

I'm already in the pilot seat, watching Waren bring us

in to make sure I can trust it, so I pull the flight belt over my torso and tighten the straps on my satchel so Seven won't get flung out if we land hard.

I feel the planet's gravity take hold, like it's trying to pull my gut out through my ass. Seven makes a worried-sounding *maow,* and I make a kissy noise for her sake, while I lean my head back and focus on my breathing.

"This landing is bullshit, Waren," I say loudly over the shuddering of the ship.

"Doing my best."

The landing thrusters kick in and my stomach goes the other way. We start to spin around slowly, and in the under-hull camera I can see the landing pad rotating smoothly and coming up to meet us. Waren drops us down so gently the landing gears are nearly silent as they touch ground.

"We have arrived."

"Thanks, Waren. You did well."

"I know, but thank you."

• • •

I leave Seven with Waren. She's *maow*ing incessantly, but I know after I've been gone five minutes she'll be curled up somewhere, sleeping.

Outside, it's like walking through a fish tank that hasn't been cleaned since, well, ever. A murky effluvium coils through the air, and even through the rebreather I can taste the fetid damp in the back of my throat.

Mold grows on every surface, black spots spreading across the landing pad and down the gangway. It looks regularly scraped, but I still slip a couple of times as I follow the gangway down into the murk, barely managing to stay upright. A flashing neon sign saying LOCAL SHOES guides me down from the elevated airfield, and I figure it's as good a place as any to start asking questions.

The winding path veers left first, then right, before straightening up and depositing me in a tiny town square, right in front of the general store/shoe emporium. There's a bar and a diner, too. It seems like those three structures make up the settlement of Sochynsky, besides any houses scattered and hidden by that constant veil of fog and the densely packed trees. The trees are swallowed by the mist, black bark making them look like shadows, spotted with disk-shaped fungi in shades of orange, purple, and green.

"Whadyoo lookig foor, mish?"

It takes me a few seconds to spot the guy, sitting on a bench to my right. The long tube from his full-face gas mask coils down to the seat beside him, attached to a burner, cooking some sort of leaf or maybe drug.

"Wanna take that thing off your face before you try talking to me?" I say, tempted to flick it off myself.

He cocks his head for a second, then he pulls the mask

off, but from the look on his face, he doesn't seem too happy about it.

"Better," I say. "I'm looking for an old friend; info I got says they came down on this side of the planet."

The guy stands up and the burner hangs from his mask, bobbing on its accordioned tube. He's got the gangly limbs and sunken chest of a kid, but he's overly tall, with wretched skin half claimed by the mold.

"If he landed on this hemisphere, then he's in Sochynsky. I can help you find him for a fee." The burner pendulums as he reaches down and pulls a ballistic rifle from where it was leaning against the council trash bin. "I'm good at tracking folks—real good."

"Gotta do this myself."

"I haven't even told you my fee," he says, lifting the mask up to his face and taking a hit of whatever it is he's burning.

He isn't holding the gun like a threat, but an ugly energy comes off him. I'd rather he was selling drugs instead of tracking services, just so I could buy some and get him off my back.

"It ain't about the creds," I say; "it's just personal business."

"If you say so," he says, with a shrug. He puts the mask back on, and I see his skinny chest swell, either because he's taking another hit or because he's getting ready to keep talking at me. I walk off in case it's the latter, and head to the general store.

The entrance to the shop is a rudimentary air lock, but inside the air is heavy with motes floating on the current from the air circulator—probably mold spores.

I find a pair of shoes in my size and take them to the counter. The shopkeeper must have as much faith in his air-filtration system as I do, because he's still wearing his rebreather inside. His skin is a sickly gray pallor that looks more like fungus than flesh. Probably everyone on the planet has the same gray skin after they've been here long enough.

"Just the shoes today?"

"Yeah, and some information too, maybe." I tap his cred terminal with a finger, as if to say *And I'm willing to pay for it*. "I'm wondering if you've seen somebody about? She's about my height and build, hair black or really dark brown. Has a tattoo like this on the back of her hand."

I draw the symbol for theta in the congealed muck on the counter:

Deep lines spread out from the guy's eyes as they squint half-shut. With his face partly hidden, I can't tell if he's thinking real hard or if I've offended him by pointing out how filthy his shop is.

After a couple of seconds he says, "Nah, I'm awfully sorry, miss; ain't seen a woman matching that description."

"What about any strangeness?" I say, trying a different tack. "Things getting knocked over or thrown around without cause? Things getting crushed? Places being blocked off?"

"Now you mention it, there has been some strangeness like that. Northwest out of town, used to be a real good spot for 'shroom picking. Few months back, it got so people couldn't find it anymore."

"You mean the mushrooms stopped growing there?"

"Nah, that ain't it. It was like you couldn't get to it no more, even if you knew where to go. You'd walk the same way you'd gone a hundred times afore, but you'd end up someplace else. You'd walk past it or around it."

"Northwest, you said?"

He punches a figure into his cred terminal. After I pay it, he says, "Yeah, maybe ten, fifteen kilometers out. It's a wide dip in the ground, a clearing where none of the big trees grow, just the mushrooms. Hold on a second." He mustn't have been offended before, because now he draws on the countertop, too, a simple map in finger smears. I take a photo of it using my ocular lens, though it'll probably be useless.

"You got nav satellites on Ergot?"

"Nah. I mean, they're out there, imperial regs and all that, but with the air how it is, signal's about as good as the emperor's word." He chuckles at his own joke.

I ignore it and say, "All right, I'll take the shoes, and I guess I need some supplies for the hike: water and food—whatever you've got that's lightweight and high in protein."

He takes down a watersack from the shelf behind him, and a couple of packs of mushroom jerky in different flavors. "You won't get there in those shoes; you'll need the boots," he says, pointing at a display with a price that's roughly triple the cost of the shoes I already picked out.

My innate dislike for being upsold kicks in and I say, "No, the shoes will be fine."

He shrugs, then rings up the bill.

CHAPTER TEN

There are a few tracks leading away from Sochynsky, trails between the tall dark trees where the moss isn't quite so thick. The HUD on my ocular implant includes a compass, so I find the trail that vaguely leads northwest and I follow it. I pass a couple of houses up high on stilts, as if the altitude would keep the damp at bay, then the trail gets overgrown with moss and different fungi.

The ground is always wet underfoot, though the dirt doesn't really turn to mud. It holds together, cohesive like a firm gel, and my footprints expand back up to meet the level of the ground a moment after I move on. For all the moisture, my feet are still dry; void bless these local shoes.

After an hour or so, I stop and lean against a tree. I have to fight the urge to pull my rebreather off, and it's a struggle to convince myself that, no, I won't be able to breathe easier without the mask over my face. I lift the rebreather up just enough to shove some jerky into my mouth, but I suck in a mouthful of damp air that makes the jerky taste like mold. For a second I worry about the spores taking root in my lungs and eating them from the inside out, but I figure if people live here, it can't be that bad—at least in small doses.

I push on, hearing the odd, plastic-sounding squelch of the ground beneath me change to a sort of hiss. Looking down, I see the earth is granular, small spheres of dark dirt being parted by my footsteps.

Ergot seems a strange place to live. For a fugitive like Sera it makes sense, but I can't think why anyone else would. There must be other 'Riph planets that are plenty private, where the government won't bother you and which aren't mold farms with barely breathable air.

While I'm wondering if there might be temperate 'Riph worlds with greenery and fresh water, I hear something above me—skittering, like an animal. It sounds too close, but visibility is practically zero, and the air between the trees is thick with vapor. I keep walking and the sound seems to follow—skitter, pause, slam—as if the animal is leaping between trees to track me.

Something hits the ground behind me and I spin around. I see what could be a shadow moving in the mist, or it could just be the haze itself shifting. I walk backward a few paces, expecting to see the air shift in whatever way air should, but the shadow moves toward me, feet pattering over the ground.

I reach out and clasp my hands together loosely to

catch the thing. As I walk toward the small prison I've made, I hear shuffling sounds and then sharp, high-pitched squeals. I move closer still and then I see it. It's a primate, covered in thick, coarse fur that looks slick like waterproofed fabric. It only reaches to about knee height, but I can tell it's an adult because it carries a sleeping young one on its back.

It stops squealing when it sees me, and for a second I think about crushing my hands together, wondering if this thing eats meat, wondering how many others are hiding in the mist, waiting to pounce. But then I see the small mushrooms in its hand and the ones it has crushed into the dirt.

I step back and release it, one hand poised to slap it away if it jumps at me. Instead, it just walks forward, sniffs the ground where my feet have disturbed the earth, and drops a mushroom down and smashes it into the wet soil.

It's farming. I watch it for a little while longer until I'm sure, then I walk on.

The primate stops following me when the dirt beneath my feet changes back to the gelatinous-type earth, sticking to its farmlands.

A few minutes on I almost miss its company, wishing vaguely that I'd brought Seven despite the risk to her tiny lungs. Then I see a bloodred mass up ahead, the color somehow seeping through the haze. It's Mount Hamilton, according to the map I downloaded on the way to Ergot, but the locals call it Blood Mountain, on account of the fungus peculiar to that area staining the whole thing a deep red.

The shopkeeper had said, "Once you see Blood Mountain coming out of the mist, you're almost there. Put the mountain at your two o' clock, then walk straight ahead. If you can."

I do as the shopkeeper said, and after a hundred meters or so I see what he was talking about. It's not like a powershield that blocks you completely, it's more gentle than that. If you stop focusing on Blood Mountain, suddenly it's over to your left and you didn't even realize you'd veered away.

I sit down, and straightaway I can feel the dampness soaking through my pants. I eat some more jerky, drink some water, then stare out ahead. I wonder whether I'd be able to see the wall in front of me if I had some Squid drops, a shimmering mass of distortion among the trees and vines.

I stand up, brush the mud off my ass, then reach my hands forward. I feel them dig into something thicker than the damp air, so I step forward and wrench my arms apart, like I'm opening curtains made of lead. My jaw tenses as I press forward, feeling the strain as I push through the psychic wall, tearing a hole in it with my mind.

I've started making a sound behind clenched teeth—my training coming in automatically—so I crank the volume and push ahead faster. I plod one foot down hard and check for purchase before I shift my weight onto it, then repeat with the other. Just as I strain against it, the wall disappears. My body jerks forward and my ankle twists painfully as I topple over.

"Fu—," I yell, the word cut short as I hit the ground, hands up to break my fall. I land soft on the thick layer of moss and fungi carpeting the forest floor, but I slip as I push up from the muck and get a wide streak of mud across the visor of my rebreather. I pull it down and leave it hanging around my neck while I carefully pick myself up into a crouch, keeping my weight off the twisted ankle. The joint throbs, swelling already, and I hear my breath coming fast and loud as my body adjusts to the pain.

I look up from my ankle and glance around. The shopkeeper was right about there being no trees growing here, but I wouldn't call it a clearing. There are rocks stained orange with rust and covered in a dense, black moss, and fallen trees lie here and there, trunks too thick for me to see over.

I know the ankle isn't broken because my medical diagnostic suite would be blaring warnings at me, so I stand slowly, arms out for balance.

"You should have paid extra for the hiking boots," a voice calls out, mirroring my own thoughts. The words echo in the stillness, and though I haven't heard her speak in fifteen years, I know it's Sera.

"Did you fucking trip me?" I call into the sky above.

"I didn't need to—the ground here is a hazard."

My hands are coated in blue-brown mud and green moss from breaking my fall. I wipe them on the ass of my pants, glad that I left my cloak behind for Seven to curl up on.

"Why the hostility, Mars?" she calls out, but this time there's less of an echo. I think I know where she's coming from.

I hold my arms apart, and my mind grabs one of the huge fallen logs.

"You tried to have me killed!" I yell. I strike out, swinging the tree like it's a twenty-meter-long club.

I hear Sera *oomph* as the wind is knocked out of her, then a body flies through the air backward, disappearing into the mist. She's quick though, and near instantly a rusted boulder hurtles close and splits my log with a sharp crack.

I hear creaking and snapping behind me, and a line of trees at the edge of the clearing start to come down all at once. I can't run, so I drop to a roll, grab another fallen tree, and hold it over me. The other trunks thud as they land on it, pushing my body down into the mud with the force.

My arms burn and begin to shake. I reach deep inside, finding that well of strength the teachers taught us would always be down there, waiting for us, waiting for our need. I tap into it and I start screaming, except instead of the guttural sound I usually make, it's the high-pitched wail of a banshee.

I throw my giant cudgel high into the air, tossing aside the fallen trees like matchsticks. They disappear into the mist, and one by one they hit the ground out of sight, cracking loudly as they land.

I stand up panting and inhale so I can yell something clever at Sera, but I hear a noise behind me, and when I spin around she's right there. The last thing I see is her knuckles rushing toward my face.

CHAPTER ELEVEN

I come to, and my head and foot are throbbing just off beat with each other. When I try to open my eyes, the right one doesn't want to cooperate. There's a migraine splitting my head just behind my left eye, but it's less from the punch and more from the mental jujitsu. The migraine is familiar, almost like an old friend—one that you actually hate, but whom you keep seeing out of some misplaced sense of loyalty—but the black eye is a new sensation, and I can't stop myself from poking at it and wincing in pain.

"Good, you're awake. Have you cooled off yet?"

I look around the room, trying to find where Sera's voice is coming from. The walls are made from a white plastic or synthetic fabric. They glow faintly, scaring the shadows away.

"Where are we?"

"This is my home. I hope you wiped your feet before coming in."

I don't remember Sera's sense of humor being so terrible, but I know she's joking because half the floor is caked in mud and the other half is covered with an ancient threadbare rug, already being eaten away by Ergot's mold.

The furniture looks as though it's made from the wood of the local trees, and the only visible metal in the prefab-kit home is the heater/oven standing in the far corner. That corner is the one place where moss and mold don't grow up the walls in constellations of black spots—the heat from the oven one final refuge against the damp.

The house is one of those portable, collapsible structures favored by nomads, the military, and, by necessity, refugees.

Sera's near the oven, slicing mushrooms. Even if the shopkeeper had seen her, he wouldn't have recognized her from my description. Her hair is gray now—light gray, nearly white—and looks like it hasn't been brushed since I last saw her, with one thick dreadlock forming in the back, and the rest of it unkempt and visibly knotted. Her skin hasn't taken on the Ergot-gray yet, but it's already paler than I remember her. The theta symbol still covers the back of her hand, moving smoothly down and up with the blade. The other arm is prosthetic now, coated in some sort of thick polyrubber to keep out the damp.

"Why did you do it?"

"Knock you out? Because I needed to calm you down."

"Not that," I say.

"Are you hungry?"

My stomach churns, but I say, "Answer the fucking question."

She *tsks*. "They didn't teach us language like that at the facility. I'm not avoiding the question, Mariam; you'll get your answers in good time. But first, are you hungry?"

"Yes," I say, quietly and begrudgingly.

"I'm making mushroom risotto. It's not great, I'll admit that much, but the rice and the mushrooms will be fresh; can't grow much else on Ergot."

She takes a few more minutes in the kitchen. Once the pot is on the stove, she comes over and takes a seat opposite me. Up this close I can see the lines on her face that go with the gray hair, and the dark pockets beneath her eyes. She looks older than she is, maybe old enough to be my mother, when there's really only six years between us. She stares and smiles.

"I want to know everything, Mars. Where did you go? How did you survive? Are you married?"

I sigh and poke my swollen eye again. "I haven't seen you in fifteen years, and you want to make small talk?"

"I want to hear what I missed, even the dumb little things." Sera gets up and goes over to a small cooler, then returns after a minute with two mugs full of a dark brown liquid.

I take a sip and it's gritty and sour, with the burn of

strong alcohol. "I got out of hibernation and waited for you for a day or so. I was sure you were dead, but I still hoped, y'know? Figured they'd be searching for a home-less kid, a runaway, so I sold myself into an Orphancorp." I drink some more of the fungus wine. "It was fucked, but it wasn't as bad as the facility. They fed me, housed me, and they move kids around to keep them from forming any bonds, which kept me off the radar."

"Smart," Sera says, still wearing the same placid smile she had on when she sat down.

I shrug. "The facility taught us to survive, how to do whatever we needed to. I've killed a lot of people, Sera. I'm not proud of it."

She nods.

"I saw you die," I say, the venom in my voice surprising me. My eyes go to the floor, away from her face despite my anger.

I hear fabric rustling and I look up. Sera's lifted her tu-nic high enough that I can see her flat, ridged abdomen. She's showing me four vivid pink scars—splashes of skin turned shiny by laserburn.

"You *did* see me die, but they brought me back," she says, lowering her shirt. She looks at me intently and I glance away, but my eyes are drawn back to hers. "It was peaceful there, being dead, I mean; it felt like a living nothingness."

"Like the inside of a wormhole."

"Exactly. They brought me back from that just so they could keep pushing me to the edge of death. At first they wanted me to talk, tell them where I'd sent you, but I didn't. Eventually it simply became punishment." She holds up the digits on her prosthetic arm. "They pulled out my fingernails. Do you know what that feels like? Do you know how hard it is to scratch without them? This arm's great though," she says, admiring it.

"If you didn't talk back then, why did you send a bounty hunter after me?"

"She was only supposed to give you a message, sis—telling you to find me here. That's it. How could I ever wish you harm? All I can guess is she put her feelers out once she had your name and found someone who was willing to pay more for you."

I'm about to ask something, but Sera holds up an index finger and goes over to the stove. After a couple of minutes she's back with two plates of risotto.

It smells good and is edible enough, but there's an underlying bitterness to the local produce that reminds me of bile, that flush of hot spit that signals an unavoidable vom. I'm too hungry to be fussy, though, and I've already eaten half of it when Sera picks up with her story.

"Between the two of us we could probably populate a cemetery planet," she says, sounding like she's idly musing. "When I escaped, I wanted to make sure they wouldn't ever be able to stick things into me and cut pieces of me away again." Now it's time for Sera to hang her head. "I wanted to murder all of them," she says, almost in a whisper.

I start to speak, but she cuts me off.

"I rigged the reactor to explode on my way out. I watched the facility detonate, watched the fire and debris spill out into space.

"I stole a ship, and I sat there and watched all the carnage floating out into the void, and I thought about all the girls who had lived there, sis. All those girls are dead, and I killed them." She doesn't mention the soldiers, the scientists, the caretakers, and I don't blame her. "That was the last time I cried. Nothing else seems worth crying over anymore."

My migraine is gone now, but I've got these weird bits of color floating in my vision.

"They lost a lot of research and all the subjects that could help them piece it back together. All but you. And me I guess, but I'm already dead. That's why they're still after you."

The whole house starts to swim, and I lose focus on Sera's face. My stomach is in agony, but I want to follow what Sera's saying.

"But why bring me here?" I ask.

"To help you, Mars, help you get strong enough to fight them."

The bowl of risotto slips out of my hand and thuds onto the rug.

"The shopkeeper—"

"Dale."

"Dale . . . When he said people came here to pick mushrooms . . . he, uh, he didn't mean for food, did he?"

"I'm sorry, Mars. I wanted to tell you first, I really did, but we'd already wasted so much time fighting. Vomit now if you're going to, because soon you won't be able to choose where it ends up."

I stand up and the whole house swings wildly backward, then forward, sloshing around like liquid reality. I can't really feel my legs, so I lift them up high as I stumble toward the door, not knowing where the toilet is in Sera's tiny house.

Outside I'm on my hands and knees, looking at a collection of mushrooms spotted with hollow purple circles, then I'm looking at mushrooms covered in risotto, then I'm looking at the inside of my eyelids, lines of . . .

CHAPTER TWELVE

Red veins run through pink, jagged lines of life. They move, vibrating gently with a heartbeat, but not mine. The veins dance with a slow, solid thud that shakes my whole body. It's my mother's heartbeat, and it's my mother's warmth that envelops me. I am home. I am not alive; am I dead? I am not yet alive; I am not yet dead. I'm pushed out of my home, into the light. The sun shines and then it winks out, goes black and cold. Another sun lives and dies, then another. Galaxies form and I float among them; I am one of them. The universe dances gently along with a heartbeat, but it is not mine. The heartbeat goes silent and all is void. All is the lack of light, the lack of dark, the lack of even a line that separates the two like the edge of shadow.

My father worries for my mother. My mother does not worry because her own fate is certain. She will die. She is dead. She has always been dead. She will never die. She will never live.

I'm five years old and they tell me I don't have parents, that I never had parents, that I was made in a lab, that I belong to them and if I don't perform as they expect, they will do away with me. Briggs kills a mouse. Cleanly, quickly, with a scalpel across its tiny throat, and then he holds it up to make sure we know what "do away with" means, so we can learn their little euphemisms.

Euphemisms gain strength by hiding the truth. Nothing is truth, nothing is reality, my mind contains multitudes, it contains universes, I contain multitudes, I am Mariam, I am Sera, I am every caretaker that ever had a hand in molding me, I am mold growing across every surface of Ergot. I am already dead because I want to die, because I have always wanted to die, because I don't deserve to live, because I am a tool without purpose, a weapon without a target.

I am a little girl. I have just emerged from a shuttle, held tightly in the arms of my sister. Held tightly in the arms of my Sera. Held tightly. My sister? Sera holds tightly on to me, and she whispers in my ear and she tells me that Daddy will be back for us, that Daddy will come find us, but I don't believe her. Sera is my sister, and they separate us. They separate us by age and they tell us we do not have families, that we never had families. Sera isn't my sister, because the tattoo on the back of her hand is different from mine. I forget her. I forget who she is. I train and I forget.

Briggs is there, watching and grinning as men in white put needles in my arms and through my skull. There is only pain, only pain and the men. They use hypnotism to rewrite the code of my brain, but it's not just hypnotism. They've opened up my skull, and wires run out of the pink-gray matter-flesh and hang in loose parabolas and meet the floor and snake until they run into a machine. This machine talks to my brain, and this machine lies to my brain and makes me need them, listen to them, obey them; but I do not need them, I need them, I am alone and I need them, because I am just a tool without purpose, a weapon without a target, and I need them because they know how to point me. I will always come home and I will never come home, because I left it, because no one would ever want me, because look at me. Look at this child with no notion of self, no goal, just a desire to flee and an ability to kill if it is required, and it is always required because this whole universe is built upon kill, the first thing they taught me was kill.

Mice were released into the section of the space station where our food was stored and prepared. The mice were released and they bred and they bred and ate bread and whatever else they could get their tiny little mouths around. They told us: you either kill the mice or the mice will eat your food. We won't stop them; you have to, or you will starve. So we did. We would run around the kitchen quarters and we would laugh and giggle and squeal and we would search on our hands and knees and we would find the mice and we would turn their tiny bodies inside out—that's what people say when there isn't really an inside for the organs and the blood to stay inside of.

They never said anything about the bodies, so we left them and we ran and laughed and giggled and found more mice, and soon the whole place smelled of death. We were a mouse holocaust and still we starved for a week while they cleaned the kitchens and the food stores and tried to get rid of that smell, though they never could, because the air can only be filtered and refiltered so much, and you can't open the windows on a space station. We starved for a week, because even though we killed all the mice, we still didn't deserve to eat, they said. We didn't deserve to live, they never said, but it was there floating in the air above their heads.

I used to sleep on the floor of my room, my cell, because I didn't deserve to sleep on a bed, because I was some hated something that hated itself and would lie on the floor and cry. Some nights I would fall asleep down there on the hard metal floor, but other nights I would get into bed because even though I didn't deserve it I wanted it and I am a little girl that gets what she wants.

They use hypnotism and science and they alter my brain and they put in these little codes so they can control me, but there are two mes. There is the little girl, skull open on an operating table, and there is this other me, this me which is a galaxy of stars and planets and thoughts. I reach into my little-girl brain. I reach in and I find the places where they broke me and rewrote me and made me hate myself more than I hated them. I find the places where they made me weak because they feared me, where they made me weak because they needed a tool, they needed a weapon. I find the weaknesses and I turn them inside out, and they bleed and they die.

The little girl lies on the operating table and I want to cry for her, but galaxies can't shed tears. Galaxies can't shed fears.

The universe is fear is death is life feeds on life feeds on the stars that circle each other in a dance performance on a scale we cannot fathom, and because we cannot fathom it we do not care. It is forever. The stars live forever, I live forever, I burn with the heat and light and destruction of a billion split atoms, I am become death, I am becoming. . . .

I am. . . .

I am.

CHAPTER THIRTEEN

"Where are we?"

I must have wandered and Sera must have followed, because we're someplace outside of the clearing, surrounded by trees stretching up to disappear in the murk.

"Are we on the other side of your barrier?" I ask.

"No . . . well, yes; we would be, but I haven't put it back up."

It's too dark to see much, but all around us the trees are spotted with bioluminescent fungus. Half the mushrooms underfoot glow as if reflecting moonlight, and blue-lit fireflies flit through the gloom; even the jacket Sera is wearing glows like the walls of her house. It seems like I'm the only thing that doesn't glow, that doesn't carry a brightness around within itself.

"I usually just stroll," Sera says, "but you were a woman possessed. Once you were done vomiting you took off."

That explains why my sprained ankle is on fire. This time I can't even be sure it isn't broken. During my fungal fugue my mediag suite switched itself off, along with my burst modem and ocular implant. On the upside, the swelling around my eye has gone down.

"Why didn't you tell me?"

"Tell you what?"

"We're sisters; you're my sister."

Sera looks at me, confused, and for a split second I feel like an idiot for believing what my 'shroom-brain told me, but then she asks, "It needed to be said?"

I try to speak, but I'm not sure how to parse everything that's going through my head. Sera must see that I'm struggling, because she steps over and hugs me. I hold on to her, maybe for too long, but she doesn't seem to mind. "I was so young when we went to the facility. I didn't remember anything from before that. They told us we didn't have family; I just thought you were my only friend in that place."

Sera smiles. "But I call you 'sis'—I always have."

"I didn't think it was literal; I thought it was a term of endearment."

"It was both."

"Where are we?" I ask again.

"Don't worry, I brought a compass. You saw it, right?"

Hypnotic conditioning, neurolinguistic de/reprogramming, an utter destruction of self-esteem and self-worth—all the threads that made up the leash the facility put around our necks.

"Yeah, I saw it."

"And you broke free?"

"Free?" I put a hand to my stomach; part of me feels like I could vomit some more, but my gut feels like a void, a vacuum. I could almost eat. "I think so? I don't know; I was busy being a galaxy, watching the universe form and die around me."

Sera laughs, but I was dead serious. "Imagine how much these things would sell for in the interior. Do you have any friends?" she asks. I wonder if Sera is planning some sort of encephallucinogen smuggling ring. I think of Squid, Mookie, and Trix, and Miguel too, but then Sera says, "Like, close friends? Long-term ones?"

"I guess not," I say.

"Me neither. No partners worth mentioning, never married, never felt like I could settle into a career job. And that got me wondering—what if they did that to us, to keep us reliant on them? So I started looking for something that might open my mind's eye—remind me of a few things I forgot." She shrugs. "That's what brought me here."

"But they wanted us independent," I say. "They wanted to be able to give us a target and know we'd go and get it done, right?"

"Yes, but they wanted us to come back. *Temporary* independence is what they really wanted."

I only notice now that Sera is carrying a bowl of

risotto, the black ceramic merging with the digits of her prosthetic arm. She eats a mouthful and I assume it's "clean." I'm about to ask for some when I see the wide black saucers of her pupils taking up most of Sera's irises, leaving only a thin sliver of green around the edges.

"How much of this stuff do you do?"

"What do you mean, 'how much'?"

"How often?"

"Not every meal," she says, "that would be ridiculous. Only dinners; sometimes lunch as well."

It suddenly makes sense—the deep lines in Sera's face, the bags under her eyes, the unkempt hair.

"Sera, you need to get help," I say.

"Why, what's wrong? Do you need a doctor?"

• • •

Sera finishes the risotto on the walk back to her glowing white house, talking around mouthfuls of masticated rice and encephallucinogenic mushrooms.

"Their end goal was to have one of us married to every system senator and the heads of all the spacer guilds. After that, Briggs would make his move and we'd explode the heads of everyone who might stand in his way."

"That would take more than the temporary independence you mentioned," I say, humoring her manic, conspiratorial madness.

"Obviously they wouldn't make that move until they knew they could control us. Control us the way they control the boys."

"But there aren't any boys."

"A eunuch can still be a boy, Mariam. Unless, of course, she's a girl."

We walk in silence—me trying to make sense of everything Sera's saying, her probably on a mushroom-fueled journey deep into her psyche—until we reach the hut. Once inside, Sera starts cleaning the dishes while I sit on the edge of her bed. She spends five minutes washing each dish, strange keening sounds coming from the back of her throat as she works.

"I need to give you something," she says, slowly scrubbing a plate.

I wait a full minute, then ask, "What?"

"What?"

"What do you need to give me?"

"That's right, I need to give you something." She finishes with the plate, dries it, and puts it away, then goes to the far corner of her house and starts riffling through a small set of drawers. She comes over, holding a shard gingerly, as though it might bite. She passes it to me and visibly relaxes as she sits beside me.

"What is it?" I ask, but then I swipe the shard to unlock it, and I know without her needing to say. "Dad?"

A man peers out of the shard, black stubble over his face and long straight black hair with a small streak of gray running from his left temple. He has gray eyes that—I swear to god—twinkle as he smiles at the camera. Behind him is forest, deep green leaves and trunks so dark they're almost black.

"Do you remember him?" I ask.

"A little, I think, but I don't know how much of it I made up just to fill in the gap between now and when I saw him last. I remember watching him get paid while they took us."

"What about our mother?"

"She looked a lot like you do now, I think. Her hair was more conservative, long and straight, but without the missing parts." My hand goes to the side of my head and I touch one of the scars that line my scalp, marking all the places they installed augs and altered my brain. "You've got her eyes, her cheeks, her mouth."

Staring at Sera, I see now that half her face is mine, disparate parts, but obvious when you know where to look.

"I remember our mother's smell, but not what she sounded like. She always smelled like fresh-baked sweet bread."

"She baked?" I ask, trying to remember something, anything.

Sera smiles, then shrugs. "I don't know; maybe it was just her shampoo." Sera cocks her head, and before I can ask her what it is, she says, "No."

I reach out and feel it in a flash: a large-caliber bullet, high velocity, aimed at my torso. I sweep the bullet aside with my right arm, and Sera does the same, our movements in unison.

I feel Sera's mental shove like a breeze. I slam it aside with the force of a hurricane. Sera is shoved into the chair hard as blood bursts from the hole in her chest.

"No," she says again, her voice calm and quiet, then the crack of rifle fire echoes into the air.

I pick his mind out, a single point of light in the surrounding sea of fog and tree.

I'm up and moving instantly, tearing the bullet hole in the plastic wall wide enough for me to run through, anger dulling the pain in my ankle as I leap over stones and fallen branches. I can see him now as he takes aim: the skinny tracker from town.

The bullet reaches me just before the sound does, and I fling it aside, hear it *chank* into a tree behind me, and then I'm on him.

"Fugg," he says, voice just as muffled even without the burner blocking the end of his gas mask.

He reloads, but with a flick I knock his rifle away, tearing his arm free as well. He screams as blood sprays the ever-wet ground.

"Why did you do it?!"

He takes rasping breaths and says, "Theh boungy." He twists his remaining arm, showing me a shard, with my face staring out of it and a price so high I can't blame him for trying. "Wasz jush tryig to woong yoo."

I hold my hand out and clasp his skull in my empty grip. I feel my mouth contort in a sneer. I'm about to clench my fist and crush him, but then I think of Sera and decide he doesn't deserve that mercy. I turn and walk quickly back to the shack, hearing his moans behind me as I leave him to bleed out.

By the time I'm back, Sera has slid onto the floor, blood spattering from her mouth and chest as she struggles to breathe. The hole is ragged, with bits of white and shades of red and pink. I kneel down behind her, put her head in my lap. She's blurred by tears when I look down at her face.

"I don't know what happened," I say. "I just tried to knock it aside; I didn't mean to—"

I wipe my eyes with the back of my hand, a streak of wet tattoo shining darker than the rest.

"Fuck. I didn't even think what might happen."

Sera smiles, her lips already turning pale. "It's okay, sis.

This is what I wanted. I've been so tired. I'm done, but there's more for you to do, sis; so much more." She moans and her mouth twitches and twists.

"It's okay to let go, Sera; just sleep," I say, struggling to keep my voice even.

"I looked for you once I got out. I wanted to give you a better life. You believe that, don't you, sis?"

"You did, Sera."

"Fleeing isn't freedom. I see that now. I'm sorry."

"Sera," I say softly. If she's gone, I don't want to bother the dead. After a few moments I check her pulse. Nothing.

She's gone. She's gone and all I can do is sit with her while she goes cold.

I always thought I'd watched Sera die, and now I have, fifteen years later.

I try to close her eyes like they do in the flicks, but the eyelids don't stay down. After trying three times it feels like desecration for me to keep going. I search her house and find an encrypted shard and some vacuum-packed bags of dried mushrooms. When I swipe the shard, the password prompt is "your birthday." I try Sera's first, because I can remember it now, as if I'd always known it, but that doesn't work. I try my own birthday, and the shard chimes as it unlocks. *Marius Teo.* I don't recognize the name, but I know it's our father: his location and a few other pieces of information about him. I copy the details onto the shard that holds his photo, then break the encrypted shard in half.

I don't cry. I know I will, but right now it seems pointless. I can sit in this plastic hovel and cry, or I can go. I can stop running, find Briggs, and make him answer for what he did to Sera.

• • •

I reset my implants and try sending a burst to Sochynsky. A burst should be able to get anywhere in the controlled galaxy, but it's limited by available bandwidth, and when you're in the middle of nowhere—on a 'Riph world covered in thick fog, and the nearest town is barely a pit stop—there isn't much bandwidth to be tapped.

I'd hoped that if an undertaker, or someone, *anyone*, could meet me halfway, then I'd at least be able to make sure they did everything right. But no one replies. I pull the door shut behind me and say, "I'm sorry, Sera; you deserved a better sister, a better life."

You spend fifteen years thinking someone's dead, then a few weeks thinking they betrayed you, then a few short hours thinking of them as family, and at the end of it all you don't know what the fuck to think. I know I'm not done grieving. I don't even know if I've started.

I walk, relying on Sera's compass and a basic idea of where I'm going. As long as I focus, I can use my mind like a crutch so I don't have to put all my weight on the injured ankle—but still, it's a long fucking walk.

CHAPTER FOURTEEN

"Who the fuck was he?" I've got the shopkeeper Dale up against the wall with my forearm across his throat. I don't want to flex my mental muscles until I know what tipped off the tracker.

"Who?"

"Scrawny kid, gun as tall as he was."

"Chet? That's Marge's kid; he's always checking the bounty boards, thinks he's gonna be a bounty hunter when he grows up."

"There ain't gonna be an 'up' for Chet," I say. "Kid killed my friend; kid's dead."

Dale's face scrunches up, like he's trying hard to process what I'm telling him and coming up short.

"He followed me into the clearing and he killed my sister. Did you know anything about it?"

"I thought you said she was your friend?" he says. I push my arm harder into his throat and he croaks, "Sorry." After a second I relax. "I had no idea, miss, but Chet's always been the type to run outside first, and then put his breather ."

I step back and let Dale breathe, then go and lean against the counter.

"I need someone to go and get both bodies."

"Ain't nobody can get into that clearing, miss."

"They can now, Dale." I get the vacuum-sealed mushrooms out of my pocket and drop them beside the cred terminal. His eyes light up seeing the bag of superpsilocybin. "Take care of Chet's body however Marge would like. I know she'll be upset about her boy, so you need to make her understand that he didn't give me a choice."

Dale just nods, eyes still on the 'shrooms. I put my cred chip on the counter.

"As for Sera's body, I'm paying enough, so I expect a proper burial," I say, "full Hunritch rites. If I find out it wasn't done properly, I'll come back here, and you don't want that."

Dale repeats "Hunritch rites" slowly to himself as he writes it down. "Would you like a recording sent to you?" I think about that for a second, wondering if I want to see it. He must think I'm being cheap, because he adds, "No extra charge."

"Okay, sure," I say, then I give him my burst code—the one I use for official communiqués, the one I took from the first bounty hunter I ever had to kill.

"How'd those shoes work out for you, miss?" Dale

asks, his face starting to lighten after the talk of killing and burials.

"Kept my feet dry, but I should have paid extra for the boots," I say, limping toward the exit.

He chuckles. "Oh, and there's someone waiting to see you. But it's not really a someone, more like a some*thing*."

"Why didn't you say earlier?"

"I sorta forgot on account of you shoving me against the wall, miss. You'll find 'em at your ship."

I wave and walk through the air lock, out into the murk.

There aren't many people who could send a *something* to pass on a message to me. If it was an emergency, maybe Miguel, maybe Squid, but more likely it's . . .

Fucking Briggs. At a distance, through the mist, the envoy almost looks like a person, and this one is even wearing a cloth uniform, badly crumpled from the time the android spent in storage, waiting for a mission. But as I get closer, it's obvious. Briggs's face softly undulates as Ergot's constant fog passes through the holo-field.

Beside him—it?—is the coffinlike drop-pod, cracked open with a few supplies stacked neatly beside it. Briggs will probably leave the android here when he's done with it—get it to do some recon, find out whom I was meeting with. I wonder what he'll make of Sera having been alive all this time, not having died in that explosion. Pondering that, I'm glad Dale offered the video.

"Mariam!" Briggs says as if greeting an old friend, the android's arms raising like it's offering a hug.

"Why don't you show your face, Briggs? Worried I'll crush it?"

There's a short pause, which gives me a partial answer. As well as controlling the flow of ultra–long-distance communication, the Trystero system can send inorganic objects between its beacons anywhere in the galaxy. Freight is restricted to two cubic meters, and the costs are exorbitant, but if you've just *got* to get an envoy to the other side of the galaxy in anything less than a couple of months it's your only bet.

"Of course I'm worried, my dear; I know what we did to you." He smiles, the hologram showing his wide mouth filled with too many teeth that are too straight, too white. "But this time, no, I'm afraid I'm not nearby; I have some pressing business to attend to elsewhere. I'm taking up the bandwidth of the nearest five planets just so I can talk to you in real time."

Which explains why no one at the settlement got my burst.

"Where are you, Briggs? Are you on your way here? Because I'd rather not wait for you on this sporeball of a planet."

"Wait for me? How delightful."

"You won't be saying that when I'm choking the life out of you."

"Oh, my prodigal daughter, how badly you must think I've wronged you."

"Can we hurry this up?" I say.

Another pause, so my words can travel the Trystero network and his words can come back. "Right to business, then. I thought I would need to give you more incentive to bring you home. I have your friends, Mariam, and they really wish you were here."

The hologram coming from the robot's neck changes—instead of the lifelike form of Briggs's fat head, it turns into a projection, wide and flat: Squid, Mookie, and Trix, strapped into dull steel chairs, lengths of leather holding them in place.

"How much luck do you think we would have trying to unlock latent psychic talent in three adults, Mariam? I'm afraid our techniques aren't much better than you remember. In fact, in some ways we've had to revert to more basic, dare I say, *barbaric* means. You can blame your friend Sera for that."

Briggs's face comes back.

"She was alive, you know, up until a few hours ago."

"We knew she was alive—thoroughly lost, thoroughly self-destructive, and not much use to us. She was powerful, yes, but you were always her better. You know that's why she stole you away from us, don't you? Not out of love, but because she wanted to hurt us."

"You really believe that, don't you?" I say. "That's sad, Briggs. Before now, I never knew she was my sister, but I never doubted that she loved me. And I've always known that she risked her life to give me my own."

"And what sort of life is that? Living out of a corvette, limping along the edges of imperial space, waiting to be found."

"It's better than being your weapon. It's a life I can call my own."

He smiles, and it's an ugly smile, a smile that is somehow disappointed and angry. "If you cooperate, perhaps I'll give you a life with true purpose, Mariam."

"Let them go first, and then I'll come to you."

Briggs laughs. "When have you ever demonstrated that you deserve such trust? No, I need them here until you're under our control. Once you come here, they will be freed. And then you will learn that *following the rules is binding oneself without rope.*"

I hear his words for what they are now—hypnotic suggestion, designed to make me follow orders. I smile, and after a pause so does his holographic face. He must take it as obedience, instead of anamnesis.

"Where will I find you?"

"You must return to where it all began."

Briggs's face flickers a moment, then disappears. The android's default head takes its place, and the machine's own intelligence must come into play, because it says, "What a beautiful day, citizen!" and wanders off through the murk, its maroon uniform fading into that ever-present green.

I climb into the small air lock of my still-unnamed ship—the *Mouse*?—and get Waren to run decontamination twice to try to clean the mold spores out of the air.

Picking Seven up from the floor of the living area, I say, "Run a thorough diagnostic, Waren—make sure nothing's been tampered with."

"I assure you I was vigilant the entire time you were gone."

I scratch Seven under the chin, and she leans into it but refuses to purr. "With root access they could convince you—"

"You allowed me to go untethered, remember?"

"You're tamperproof?"

"More or less. It would take more processing power than what's contained inside an android envoy to damage me."

It takes a few solid minutes of petting Seven for her to forgive me for leaving her behind. I take her through to the cockpit and leave her on my lap.

"If you don't mind, Waren, I want to do some flying."

"Of course, Mars," he says, but I note a sliver of dissatisfaction in his tone. I feel for the guy—shit, digital entity; try not to anthropomorphize, Mars—but flying helps me think, and I've got to work out my next steps.

Now that Briggs isn't choking the comms, I get a burst from Miguel as soon as we clear Ergot's gravity well. He says almost half the rioters on Aylett were arrested and hauled away, so he's checking up on me, making sure I haven't died or been captured. I burst him the rough location of my childhood "home" and ask him to find the exact coordinates, then get eyes on scene. He's so glad to hear from me after days of silence he doesn't even bring up his fees right away.

CHAPTER FIFTEEN

It's time to talk about wormholes. You can open a wormhole anywhere you want, but you've got to remember it's a two-way street. Say you put a massive drill onto the front of a ship, burrow into the center of a planet, and then hole out into space. You do that, and the vacuum at your destination is going to leak through to the core of the planet. Where you had a crappy old planet, now you've got yourself a nice new asteroid field. You could skip the drilling and wormhole from space into the planet's core, if you were feeling suicidal or if you had loyal troops. It's against every space-faring treaty ever drafted, but it's possible. Hell, it's been done. Remember Carmen-7? Largest terrorist strike in eighty years.

To prevent all that, there are minimum safe distances, or MSD. In any decently busy system, MSD with all that compounded traffic pushes you out to the edges. You can safely hole from the outer edge of one system to the outer edge of another, thousands of light-years away, near instantaneously . . . but, you've still got to get from that edge to anywhere worth a damn, and that's what takes time.

All of this is to say that just because Briggs told me to meet him where it all began, it doesn't mean he's there already.

It takes Miguel a day to find the coordinates for the old facility. It hung at the Lagrange point between the two moons of a gas giant in the Sixen system, given extra protection by an asteroid belt that orbits beyond the second of the two moons. It takes him another day to get a drone there.

A few days later, I'm still heading out from Ergot, well past minimum safe distance but gliding along without a plan, when Miguel's drone autobursts me. MEPHISTO ships have arrived. In the images it sends I spot Briggs's flagship, two Ellis cruisers, and three frigates that are too small and blurry to make out.

I pace around the cargo area of the *Mouse* with Seven asleep in my hood. I pull her out and hold her up in front of my face. She looks at me like she'd rather be sleeping.

"I've got a corvette, an AI, a weird cat-thing, and no weapons," I say to Seven, using a problem-solving trick that engineers have relied on for hundreds of year. "I've got to go up against six ships to rescue three friends. All right, three *people,* but they're people who wouldn't be in this shit if it wasn't for me."

Seven *maow*s.

"I don't think so."

She *maow*s again, louder this time.

I sigh and think for a second. "Holy shit; that might work."

I drop Seven to the floor and she rushes off, heading toward her food. I go in the opposite direction, to the cockpit.

"Waren, what's the densest mass we can get to in under three days?"

. . .

The ship shudders violently as I check the drone feed one last time to make sure nothing has changed. The six ships float there, asteroids occasionally drifting into frame, blocking the view from the drone's hiding place.

The hull of the *Mouse* creaks and strains, and a proximity warning blares through the cockpit audio.

"I thought I told you to silence that fucking noise."

The sound dies, and I just hope the fucking headache it gave me is temporary.

"Sorry."

I exhale. "You're untethered, Waren, and I trust you. So just keep us out of harm's way and keep that siren quiet. Are the wormhole coordinates locked in?"

"Yes, the coordinates are still locked in. They have remained locked in since the first time I told you they were ready."

My stomach is churning, and some part in the back of my head is telling me *You hardly know these people; you don't owe them anything,* but I know it's not true. The very least I owe them is to keep them out of my bullshit, not to get them killed.

I try not to think about how they could already be dead, murdered the moment Briggs cut the connection. But I feel like I know him well enough; he might not be planning on letting them go, but he'll keep them alive until he's had a chance to torture me with them.

"All right, punch it."

I feel the hum of the ship vibrate my bones as the stars beyond the viewscreen split open and blossom like stellar flowers, then wink out of existence. Or, rather, *we* do.

I exhale. "This is fucking stupid, Mars," I say. "Waren, keep us in the wormhole until I give the signal, just like we discussed."

"Affirmative."

"You stay here, Seven." I spin my cloak around, then hold on to the hood. With Seven inside I lift the whole thing over my head and put it on the still-warm pilot's seat.

I walk slowly through to the air lock, put on the space suit that smells like someone else's sweat, and cycle through the doors.

Spacewalking in a wormhole isn't the same sensation as when you go out into regular space. In regular space you know that if something happens to your grav boots or your tether, you'll be left drifting out there, and if someone in the ship isn't quick on their feet, you'll be about to experience one of the most horrifyingly *alone* deaths you can imagine. In worm space, there's not really any "there" there. There's no place for you to drift out into and become lost in. There's no time, there's no space. I don't know what would actually happen if you drifted off. Could you come back and intersect regular space at some unknown place? At some unknown time? It'd take brains smarter than mine to figure that out . . . or one reckless moment of experimentation.

I swing out into the nonspace and climb up the handholds until I'm on *Mouse*'s roof. I connect two tethers to the handholds behind my ass, and I watch. I stare out into the abyss, and, like always, I feel it staring back at me.

"All right, abyss, is it time? Am I ready?"

I'll never be ready.

"Waren, ready when you are."

It doesn't reply, but suddenly we snap back into real space and my vision is blocked out in large swathes of black and gray and blue, with a smattering of brown streaking across the black. The colors solidify, gain resolution, become stars, asteroids, and moons drifting off in the distance—and around us, the ships.

We come through into regular space right in the middle of Briggs's fleet, bringing with us the fury and crushing power of Brindock-13, the densest black hole in the 'Riph. We'd been kiting its edge, thrusters on full just to keep us free. We got so close it would have been impossible to escape its gravity without the wormhole to take us thousands of light-years away.

The black hole's gravity seeps out behind us, its immense power barely registering for us because we've been in it so long, but instantly taking hold of the three smaller frigates. One of them crumbles in on itself, engines and ammunition exploding, gases and flames hissing out into the void. The second lists hard to the side, then spins on a wide flat axis, suddenly lost to the gravity of the nearest moon. The third frigate tries to pull away, but its thrusters aren't strong enough; it's shoved backwards, then flips instantly and plows forward—pushed by its engines and pulled by the new alien gravity into one of the cruisers, enveloping both in silent destruction as debris spills into space.

As gravity settles the second cruiser and Briggs's flagship begin to turn toward me. The *Mouse* is too small to take a hit from one of their railguns without being vaporized, but luckily they want me alive. Short-range fighters scuttle from their hangar bays like wrathful bees, ready to engage. I reach out toward the asteroid belt, feel the spinning rocks in my grasp stop their orbit around the distant star, and pull.

The asteroids come streaking toward us, and I guide them one by one, my eyes flashing across the expanse to track them. I send a dozen hurtling into the cruiser, and they punch through from one side to the other, sending blood and bodies into space. I fling more asteroids into the swarm of fighters, and the nimble ships dodge and weave before shattering in the hail of space rocks, taking their pilots with them.

More fighters blast through the impromptu asteroid storm, heading right for me and the *Mouse*. I reach out, grab, and crush them. The ships implode, condense, become metal asteroids with human souls at their cores.

I'm yelling and I don't even know when I started. But I'm not tired; no headache builds behind my eyes. No, the only things behind my eyes are images of Sera, of the mice, of the girls—all dead because men must have their weapons.

I turn the next wave of fighters inside out, metal hulls cracking open and pilots lost to the vacuum, spinning wildly on untrackable trajectories. I leave them. I want them to suffer out there in space.

Emergency escape pods jettison from the cruiser as it leaks atmosphere in whitish plumes. I yell some horrifying glossolalia from deep in the pit of my self and reach out to crush the listing remains of the ship, catching some of the fleeing pods in the psychic maelstrom. Explosions glow orange through its crumbling hull as I compact it into a near-perfect sphere. Squid would be proud.

With the view ahead of me clear of everything but debris and the dead, I grab more asteroids as the flagship turns slowly to face me. I see the hangar bays along its side, shimmering with the subtle glow of powershields, and I send the asteroids against the hull just above these openings. The shield mechanisms fail, and the atmosphere inside starts to vent. I send the next bombardment into the hangar and feel it splitting and shattering as it cripples fighters and turns countless pilots and engineers into mince.

I'm a spacewitch, I'm a goddess of death and destruction, and I start to laugh thinking of the look on Briggs's face. *You think you know what you did to me? You don't know the half of it.*

"Waren, take us in, leech it. Make sure we hurt them when we leave."

"Yes, Mars. I've found schematics for the Mastodon-class ultraheavy capital ship. Assuming MEPHISTO has not made too many alterations to the default design, I will be able to guide you to the brig."

Briggs's brig. Of course that's where I'll find the crew of the *Nova*.

CHAPTER SIXTEEN

I leave the space suit in the *Mouse* and put my cloak back on. If I had to explain myself I'd say that the flowing fabric makes it easy for soldiers to miss when they shoot at me. The truth is it reminds me of Sera, reminds me of the one time someone gave a fuck about my life.

I try to take Seven out of the hood so I can leave her on the *Mouse,* but she refuses to let me go without her, making this vicious howl and digging her claws deep into my back. If she knows what could happen, she's not scared. Fuck, *I'm* scared, but I guess a lack of metacognition is good for something.

"We're approaching the flagship now," Waren tells me. "Counterintrusion defenses are military-intelligence level and well beyond my ability to influence. I'm afraid I will be unable to provide anything more than verbal assistance once you're on board."

"That's fine, Waren. You just give me directions to the brig, and I'll take care of the rest."

A hollow metallic thud echoes through the *Mouse,* and I hear the cutters go to work, sparking loudly on the other side of the air lock. When you can't use an existing hangar or dock, you can always make your own.

I wait in the air lock, wearing a lightweight breathing apparatus in case my impromptu asteroid-flinging display did more damage than I wanted. I brace myself, and the air lock door parts like the lens of an ocular implant, but there's no hiss of atmosphere escaping, no loss of gravity.

"Oxygen levels appear stable, but I would still advise you to take the breather with you," Waren says, as if I'm not already wearing it.

"Yes, Mom," I say, then stow the breather in my satchel as I step out of the *Mouse* and into the MEPHISTO flagship.

Waren must understand sarcasm, because he ignores that comment and continues, saying, "I'm adding a navigational overlay to your HUD. If the ship differs from the schematics, I'll do my best to make educated guesses on your behalf."

I don't respond; I'm too busy waiting for an ambush. I half expected a welcoming party waiting for me, but the corridor is empty—another benefit of making your own dock. The only light is the faint orange glow coming from panels in the corner of the floor and the spinning red of the emergency lights.

The ship is so silent that I wonder for one stupid second if it's actually in vacuum, and I force myself to inhale deeply just to be sure. I hear air whistling in through my nostrils, sharp and loud. I stomp my foot, but the floor is covered in a spongy, polyrubber matting and doesn't have the clanging resonance of most ships.

Waren's overlay paints a line along the floor, drawn in turquoise to stand out against the orange and red lighting. It pulses to show me the direction I should be heading, so after one more glance around, I move off and follow it.

The brig is located on the upper levels of the ship, the hangars on the lower. As I creep through the corridors looking for a vertilator, I'm trying to convince myself that the reason I'm not coming up against any opposition is because they're all down in the hangars, helping the wounded, putting out fires, that sort of thing. But my gut is telling me to worry, and I always listen to my gut.

I find the vertilator after a few more minutes of quiet stalking through the ship's corridors, and there's a cab waiting for me when I hit the CALL button.

The ascending metal cube moves so fast I feel inertia even through the artificial gravity. The ship is gargantuan, and all I can do while I wait is stare at its designation written in relief on the doors—MEPHISTO FLAGSHIP RAMPART, MASTODON-CLASS—and try to tamp down the anxiety that's telling me the vert has stopped, that I'm trapped and they're coming for me.

"Am I still moving, Waren?"

"Yes. Soon you will disembark onto the central concourse. From there, proceed to an upper-level vertilator to either your left or right."

Seven climbs out from the hood of my cloak and takes up a position on my shoulder. I don't know what she's expecting, but she perches, oddly heavy in that way experimental-cat-things are when they put all their weight on their tiny paws. I pull the hood up over my head, taking momentary refuge beneath it.

I feel the deceleration in the soles of my feet. I breathe in and hold a hand out, ready.

The vertilator *dings* cheerily and the doors slide apart.

The ambush I've been expecting is here. The first trooper must be hungry for promotion, because she's standing right in front of the doors with some sort of hovering weapon platform, shaped like an armor-plated pram. Behind her are a hundred troopers in maroon, with more weapon platforms, shocksticks, and other nonlethal deterrents.

Seven reacts before I can, leaping off my shoulder and straight onto the trooper's face. The woman screams and twitches, and I'm flung backward into the vertilator wall with a thud.

I slide to the ground and reach out, grab the weapon platform, and crush it, then fling it into the woman's chest as Seven bails. The woman is pinned to the ball, and both go backward at high speed. While other troopers watch the carnage tear through their ranks, I get up and run out of the vertilator screaming.

Seven's moving too. I hear her yowling off to my right, and a tiny part inside me feels fondness for that crazy animal; the rest of me is pure hatred and fury.

More of those weapon platforms fire at me, and I hold up my arms to block the force. As I neutralize the blasts or deflect them back, it feels like Sera's shield on Ergot. I barely have time to think about what that could mean—artificial psychic abilities?—before I crush the platforms and bring them to orbit around me like a shield.

With their main weapons out of action, the troopers start rushing me, yelling war cries and epithets like "void-witch" and others far worse. I push the balls out to a wider arc and turn in circles as I walk forward to keep every angle in view, remembering the dances they taught us and improvising as I go. This is stand-up tragedy; this is the free jazz of destruction; this is interpretive death.

Minutes later, any troopers that haven't fled are on the ground, either unconscious or groaning feebly—all but one. He's on his ass, scooting back as quickly as he can, as Seven prowls forward, hissing at him.

I make a kissing sound at her, and after hesitating she

comes back to my side, climbs up my body, and perches on my shoulder.

"I ... ah ..." the guy on the floor stammers. I just laugh, then pick him up and toss him over my shoulder.

I walk to the other set of vertilators; the floor is sticky beneath my feet: more blood than I expected, especially since I didn't go full-murderous on them.

I'm holding back, because after destroying five ships and an untold number of fightercraft, maybe I've killed enough people today. The sad truth is, it's too easy to take a life. You get caught up in the moment, you feel angry or threatened, and all you need to do is reach out and they're dead. Later on it can be hard. MEPHISTO taught us all kinds of tricks to minimize the guilt, to keep us soldiering on without too many emotional issues, but that's not who I want to be if I can help it, if it isn't already too late.

I turn around inside the vert, hit the button for the prison level, and look down at my footsteps, printed in blood.

The doors close. We're going up.

CHAPTER SEVENTEEN

I track blood through the upper level for a few meters until my soles dry. This part of the ship is quiet, and as I listen to my heart thumping loudly in my chest I can't decide which I prefer: the eerie silence or the exploding carnage of a one-sided melee.

It takes Waren a few minutes to reroute me past a wall that isn't on the schematics, bisecting what should be a huge, cavernous room. Seven and I are forced into some tight corridors that zig and zag. I'm sure that without Waren I'd never find my way out.

Going through these corridors, I feel like a rat in a maze. I feel like I'm a kid again and I'm being told to find some white mice, except this time I'm *not* trying to kill them.

When I reach the brig, the door slides open silently on an unseen apparatus. I creep through the door. The guard post is on the lower level, a box about two meters per side, with waist-high counters topped with vidscreens and security consoles. Past the post is a stairwell up to the gangplank that provides access to the cells. I crouch-walk into the guard post and sneak up behind the trooper sitting there, nervously tapping the counter while she reports to her superior via comms.

"The prisoners are secure; no movement on this level. Yes, sir, I'll keep you apprised of any developments."

If she weren't distracted, she'd see me creeping up behind her on the vid feeds. I tap her on the shoulder and she spins around, but shock keeps her from reacting. I grip her around the throat and her eyes go wide. She thinks I'm killing her, but really I'm just putting her to sleep.

She collapses to the floor and the sound brings out another guard. He bellows and charges me. I grab him by the throat, too, but harder this time, and I pick him up off the ground.

The amount of force it takes to lift someone off the ground is also enough to crush their windpipe or snap their neck if you don't use finesse. What I like to do is hold them around the waist at the same time; you get the full terrorizing effect for anyone else who happens to be watching, with less chance of accidental death.

I drop the guy aside once he stops squirming and walk up the stairs. I find Squid first, and they smile, like they've been waiting patiently for me to turn up.

"You took your time," they say, words distorted and crackling behind the shimmering powershield.

"I thought you could do with some more time to meditate."

On hearing Squid's voice, Seven pops her head out of my cloak and *maow*s.

"Just wait a second, little one," I say.

I punch a button on the outside of the cell, and the powershield fades away. Squid has taken a minor beating in custody, and looking at the healing split on their lips I put a hand to my own eye, though the swelling has gone down since I left Ergot. There's a split in my eyebrow that's still healing, but I kind of hope it scars, just so I've got something from Sera to carry around with me—something to go along with the cloak and bracelet she gifted me all those years ago.

"I have some bad news," Squid says. They offer a hand to Seven and she sniffs it, then rubs her chin along Squid's fingers. After a few soft purrs, she goes back in my hood. "They took Mookie away a few hours ago."

"What? Where to?"

"I heard them mention a military tribunal."

"How long ago? Could he still be on the ship?"

"I don't know," Squid says, and suddenly I'm worried that Mookie might have been caught up in my tide of carnage. I deliberately avoided the prison level, but if he was elsewhere on the ship . . .

"Waren?"

"I've been listening. Already checking transfer manifests." There's a pause and Squid looks at me expectantly.

I hear metal hammering from the next cell and walk a couple of steps to see Trix pounding on the wall with her prosthetic fist. "Let me out!" The guards let her keep her arm this time—probably because the ship walls are tougher to punch through than a portable prison.

"Apologies," Squid says, then strides over and hits the button to open her cell.

"Trix, just calm down," Squid says.

Trix doesn't listen. She crosses the distance between us, and I let her grab me by the throat. She pulls back her prosthetic hand, clenched in a glossy fist.

"This is your fault!" she yells. I can feel her whole body trembling, muscles oscillating at the frequency of rage.

"A personnel shuttle departed the flagship approximately two hours before we arrived. I didn't track any Ethric-class vessels in the system when we arrived, so I infer that Mookie was not caught up in the fight."

"You killed him with your voidwitch bullshit just getting here, didn't you?"

"He's alive," I croak, "they took him before I got here."

Trix scowls at me, but she loosens her grip. "Good."

It's not good that Mookie is on the way to some military prison fuck-knows-where, but I didn't kill him, and for now that's enough.

"Where is he?" Trix asks, the venom in her voice suggesting it's my fault Mookie's gone, and I guess it is.

"I don't know. First things first: we've got to get you out of here, then we worry about Mookie," I say, not mentioning the part of my plan where I'm going to stay behind and kill Briggs.

"You—" Trix starts, but Squid puts a hand on her shoulder.

"She's right. We can't find Mookie if we're dead."

"Let's get out of here, then," Trix says. She bashes my shoulder as she pushes past, and under her breath she says, "Always said she was bad news."

I don't argue. Squid and I follow her down the stairwell.

"Would you like me to fly the *Mouse* a little closer?" Waren asks in my earpiece while I watch Trix strip a laser pistol off one of the unconscious guards.

"No, stay where you are, Waren; we need you where leeching will do the most damage. I'll get us all there, just give me a nav line back."

"You'll be going back the way you came; I don't see any faster routes."

Trix takes the second guard's pistol and gives it to Squid, but they look at the weapon like they'd rather hold lava.

"I know you want to charge ahead and get revenge,

Trix," I say, "but it'll be better if I lead the way."

Trix stops and waves me forward.

I guide us through the tight corridors, pausing to peer around each corner. We make it to the huge room, and I'm halfway across when I hear an electronic hum to my right. I stop and turn to look. The wall Waren didn't have on his schematics is sliding down, revealing the shimmering whitish glow of a powershield just behind it.

"Quick, go go go!" I yell-whisper to the others. Squid rushes across to take cover in the far corridor, but Trix stops behind a steel column and preps her weapon.

"Mariam," Briggs says, loudly enough to be heard over the shifting barrier, "on behalf of MEPHISTO, I am delighted to welcome you home."

The wall has come down far enough to show Briggs behind the powershield, flanked by a cadre of elite soldiers. Most of them are armed with laser rifles, but a couple have their hands resting on the same weapon platforms as they had on the central concourse. There are four women standing by Briggs, unarmed, body language taut and ready, like they're about to rip us apart with their hands . . . or maybe their minds? I see something of myself in them, but that can't be: all those girls are dead. Sera was sure of it.

The wall settles with an echoing thud.

"This was never my home," I say loudly, my voice rebounding off the high ceiling.

"But we understand you here, Mariam, better than anyone else could."

I take a step toward the shield wall. "I doubt it, Briggs; I'm only just starting to understand myself. You saw what I did out there, right?"

"Very impressive, Mariam, very impressive indeed. We have never seen anything like that before. My AI is near useless at the moment with all its processors busily calculating your destructive force. Tell me, Mariam, how did you do it?"

Got seriously fucked up on encephallucinogens and watched my life and the life and death of the entire universe unfold behind my eyes? Saw what your training did to my brain and broke it apart, put it back together as it needed to be? Used a thousand years of thought to mold my brain into something better? Fuck, I'm *not even sure.*

"You wouldn't believe me if I told you."

He chuckled. "True, which is why we'll have to run the tests, Mariam. Now, if you'd be so kind as to get down on your knees and place your hands behind your head with your fingers interlocked?"

I'm standing right in front of the powershield now. Behind my back, I've got my thumb and finger wrapped around the bracelet from Sera. I cock my head to the side and smirk at Briggs.

"You saw that carnage and you still think I'm going to come along quietly? You must be dumber than that suit makes you look."

His face stays mostly pleasant, the stab at his appearance only registering as a brief tug on the corner of his mouth. Still, he can't stop his hand from running down the front of his gray dress jacket, paneled with MEPHISTO maroon and adorned with medals of his own design.

"If you don't comply," he says, "I'll lower the shields and kill your friends." He points over my shoulder, and the troops with the guns point their weapons as if they're all puppets on Briggs's strings.

I inch my foot forward and it slides through the powershield, that familiar sensation tingling up my leg.

I reach behind my head like I'm going to do what I'm told, but instead I flip Seven out of my hood and she lands on the floor and starts hissing—whether at the shimmering powershield or at me for being so rude, I'm not sure. It's enough of a distraction to drag the eyes of the troopers and Briggs's women away from me, giving me a brief window to get past the shield. Briggs is the only one who sees me step through, the smile dropping away as his face turns to horror.

I reach out to grab Briggs, but something blocks me.

"Kill the others!" he yells, pushing backward through his honor guard.

I hear the shield behind me go silent, and the troopers with the laser rifles open fire. The hall lights up with white beams flashing past me, the air awash with heat. The guns sound like banshees humming, but once I start yelling I can't hear them. I focus on the soldiers, their faces frozen in grim resolve as they take aim at the people behind me. Then there are no faces, no soldiers, just clouds of blood and gore that seem to hang in the air before artificial gravity takes hold and they fall and puddle on the ground.

Of the dozen soldiers who opened fire, there are only two left. One of them is quick enough to swivel his hovering weapon to face me. He fires, and I knock the psychic blast aside, then fling his machine and him and his buddy into the wall, where the two men break wetly against the steel. They fall lifeless to the floor, right beside the dented and smoking wreck of the weapon platform.

I turn around to check that Squid and Trix are okay. Trix's prosthetic arm is a hanging mess of melted plastic and steel, but otherwise they're both intact—physically at least. On Squid's face is the look of someone who just watched a squad of soldiers get turned into puree by a howling spacewitch monster.

"This isn't going to pan out the way you want, Briggs," I say to the man now cowering behind his assistants.

Seven makes a bizarre yowling noise, and I glance at

her, but she seems fine; probably the smell of all the blood has gotten to her. Then I hear something else. A high-pitched keening coming from the weapon platform—the one I didn't toss into the wall.

I take a step toward it and Briggs steps backward, shadowed by his women.

"What is this thing?" I ask.

"We make them here on my ship."

I'm standing beside the machine. There's no mistaking the sound now: it's a child.

"The boys were always too volatile," Briggs says. "This way we can have them produce a psychic blast on demand."

There's a lip running around the top of the machine, so I stick my fingers into the gap and feel along until I find a release. The rubber seals crack apart, and I'm hit by the condensed smell of humanity, that cooked-meat smell of hot sweat.

The boy looks maybe nine years old. He has wires running into his skull, a breathing tube in his nostrils, feeding tube in his mouth, and an IV in his arm.

"It's not as bad as it looks; they want for nothing in there," Briggs says. I turn on him so fast my cloak whips through the air. Briggs just says, "Girls," and I'm suddenly stopped.

The four of them fan out around me, their hands

reaching forward, fingers twitching as they clutch me with their minds. I feel the ground move from beneath my feet as they lift me into the air.

Trix must fire a shot, because a flash of laser barely misses Briggs. One of the spacewitches flings an arm out, and I hear Trix yelp, then a thud.

"They're women, you asshole, not girls," I say. "And they're too fucking old."

"Whatever do you mean, my dear?" Briggs says.

"The facility was destroyed. All those girls are dead."

"Ah," Briggs says, sounding happy now that I'm subdued. "Sera told you about that before you killed her, did she?"

"You killed her, not me. If you'd left me alone, she'd still be alive, she'd be happy."

"Would she? I gather she felt extremely guilty over the deaths of all those promising children. But perhaps her guilt was well earned. Even though we managed to evacuate the command staff, the researchers, and most of the girls, many still died—soldiers, support staff, maintenance workers."

"You talk about Sera's guilt, but I bet you've never lost sleep over what you did to us."

"Of course not."

"I'm going to enjoy killing you, once I'm done with these four," I say, motioning to the women.

"You lecture me about my crimes, but you're ready to kill these girls? I want you to see something, Mariam; Synthia, show her," Briggs says.

One of the women turns the back of her hand to face me. *Xi.*

"You two are practically sisters." Briggs smiles, properly this time, white teeth and too-red gums.

"I had a sister," I say. "Her name was Sera."

Briggs is about to respond, but I push out hard and drop to the floor as the women stumble backward. I pick myself up and Seven yowls as she jumps onto Synthia. The other three reach out to hurt me, and I can feel the adrenaline and the anger in their thoughts. Seven gets a good scratch across Synthia's face, but then the space-witch throws her off. Seven tries to extend her membrane to slow her flight, but Synthia lashes out with her mind and hurls Seven through the air.

"No!" I scream. I clench my fist and Synthia's head implodes, blasting a streak of red and pink and skull across the floor, but I'm not fast enough. Seven hits the wall with a yelp.

I'm screaming again, and the minds of the other three women dance in the air in front of me, trying to get a hold. Briggs runs for the corridor at the far end of the hall. I ignore the women for a moment and throw out both my hands, planting a barrier with my mind. It feels as solid as Sera's wall on Ergot, and when I lower my arms it stays in place. I feel Briggs hit the wall, like a spider feels a bug in its web.

Behind me, the women continue the attack, their assault like a weight on my mind, like the pressure of strong gravity, like the pain in your lungs as your oxygen runs out and you're breathing in carbon dioxide. I spin to face them, all standing together. Their attack peaks, a violent wave of psychic energy that I brush aside with one hand.

"You are nothing!" I yell, lifting the women off the floor, but it's not them I'm yelling at, not really. How can I yell at someone who doesn't even register in my vision, in my thoughts? They might be orbiting around me a meter off the ground, but I don't see their faces. I see Sera's face. I see girls from my childhood. Maybe I knew these three, but I don't know them now; I don't know anyone who would follow Briggs willingly. I see the boy, shivering inside a machine of death, and I see all the ones I killed downstairs. And I see my father and that fucking smile on his face in the picture, and I try to picture my mother, but it's just Sera again.

My whole body throbs. Pulses of energy rush through as the power builds inside me, clear and bright. Mind open, thoughts endless. Arms out, palms up, vision shimmering as reality burns.

The women are gone, and I'm not even sure what I did

to them. The floor is covered in blood, but the floor was already covered in blood.

I stand and walk to the corridor where Briggs is trapped, hitting my wall with one fist. He's slowing down, like he's already given up.

"This is what you wanted, wasn't it? For me to come home?" I ask.

"You are my greatest achievement, Mariam."

"You say that as if I'm not about to kill you."

He smiles, and I can't tell if it's the smile of a man who still has an ace up his sleeve, or the smile of a man who lived to see his child become exactly what he always wanted.

"It doesn't matter what you do to me," he says. "There are others, Mariam. The MEPHISTO command structure has inbuilt redundancies. Other men like me, with other projects. Other weapons like you. Nothing will change."

"I don't care," I say. "I'm doing this for me."

"Nothing will change," he repeats.

I flick my fingers and Briggs's head disappears. His torso topples forward as bits of brain and skull streak down my mental wall, falling to the ground all at once when I pull the barrier down.

I fall to my knees and struggle to catch my breath, staring at Briggs's corpse. I don't even react when I feel a hand on my shoulder: Squid crouching down beside me.

My head turns away from them. It's half because of the migraine that's throbbing inside my skull and half from shame at what they just saw me do.

"Let's go," they say, resting the gun on the floor.

They stand and offer me a hand, and I can barely get up even with the help, but after a few seconds I'm steady on my feet.

I walk back to the open weapons platform and pull the tubes out of the boy's arm, nose, and mouth. I leave the wires in his head, just in case, but tear them out of the machine. Then I lift him free. He weighs practically nothing, his pale skin stretched over tiny bones like a living skeleton.

"I'll help," Squid says, coming to join me.

"No, it's okay, I've got him. Grab Seven, please."

"She's dead, Ma—"

"Just grab her," I snap.

Squid cradling Seven, me carrying the boy, and Trix with her prosthetic arm nearly scraping the floor, the five of us must look like war refugees, blood spattered and variously broken. In a way, that's exactly what we are. Displaced, refusing to stop because stasis is death.

Waren pings my HUD softly and his nav line glows. I follow it home.

• • •

Passing back through the central concourse, I feel sick looking at all the steel balls scattered across the floor—compressed tombs for the boys I didn't even know were inside. It feels like murder.

We head down the next vertilator, back toward the *Mouse.* "Nearly there," I say as we reach the hallway where Waren parked the ship. I'm about to step around the corner when Trix hisses at me, still sounding angry.

"This is too easy, Mars."

I'm sticky with blood, Seven is dead, and Trix's arm is melted; I'm not sure I'd call it "easy," but I know what she means.

I crouch behind the corner, resting the boy on my knee. I lean forward to peek, but the migraine I'd been ignoring spikes again. I exhale, force the pain down, and look. The hum of laser batteries builds, and I pull my head back just as a beam of laserfire shoots past. The corridor explodes with light and noise as all the waiting troopers open fire.

"Fuck," I say. "Fuck fuck fuck."

"Just do your thing," Trix says, edge of irritation to her voice.

"I'm fucking spent," I say, a little too harshly. "I've caused a lot of carnage today."

"I shouldn't have dropped that gun. . . ." Squid starts to say.

"Waren, we can't reach you."

"I've got your location. You're near a void-proof blast door."

It takes a second for me to realize what it's suggesting. "If you do that, how will we get to you?"

"The *Nova* is impounded in a tertiary hangar on the underside of the *Rampart*."

The laserfire stops, and I wonder how long we've got before they charge from cover. "How do you know that?"

"I've been doing some digging while I wait for you. I heard the ship's AI was too busy to keep me out."

"All right, do it, then lead us to the *Nova*. We'll meet you in the void. Waren, if we don't make it, go and do whatever it is an untethered AI with its own ship and a galaxy to explore wants to do."

"I will, Mars; if this doesn't work, it's been a pleasure."

Past the soldiers, somewhere out of sight, Waren disengages from the hull. As he takes a circular piece of it with him, the corridor howls with the high-pitched whistle of escaping atmosphere. I hear the first of the soldier's screams, then the blast door slams closed.

"All right," I say, pushing off the wall and heading back the way we came. "Waren's going to get us to the *Nova*."

. . .

We ride the vertilator down to the lowest level, listening to the creaks and shrieks of a ship struggling to stay whole. The boy in my arms starts to squirm and moan, as if he were the ship, but then he goes quiet and I have to hold his mouth up to my ear to feel his breath.

"We're running out of time," Squid says. I know they're talking about the ship, but I'm so fatigued I can't help but take it personally.

"Sorry," I say. "We're nearly there."

People in MEPHISTO uniforms run past us in both directions, but they don't try to stop us; they barely spare the time to glance at us as they run to their emergency stations or maybe to the lifeboats.

The occasional system broadcasts have been replaced with a constant, deafening siren, but we don't need to talk. I follow Waren's directions and the others follow.

The foot traffic dies off completely before we hit the tertiary hangar. The *Nova* stands against one wall, and I've never been so happy to see a beat-up old tug. There's the outline of dock doors on the floor beneath it, and a crane arm to hold it in place when the doors open.

"Einri, do you copy?" Squid says. I'm out of the circuit, so I don't hear the AI respond. "Can you access the docking mechanism? Good. Open the door, warm up the engines, and prepare to get us all out of here."

I stop for a second, turn, and rest my head on Squid's shoulder.

"Come on," they say quietly. "Let's go."

I lift my head and see I've marked Squid's shoulder with blood and sweat. Maybe a couple of tears, if I'm honest. I look at their face as green and blue chromatophores drift beneath the skin.

"Okay."

We stagger in through the *Nova*'s opening air lock. I strap the boy into a seat in the hold. After looking down at him for a few seconds I realize Squid is standing behind me, still holding Seven in one arm.

I move over to the far side and watch out the port as the *Nova* drops out into space. My stomach churns as we leave the artificial gravity of the *Rampart* and Einri gets the *Nova*'s centrifuge spinning, and I feel a slight pull as we move away at speed. Soon we've got a view of all the carnage: two Ellis cruisers and three frigates crippled or destroyed, dozens of lost fighters, a flagship badly battered, and countless dead. So many corpses lost among the stars, so much glittering shrapnel.

It's almost beautiful.

CHAPTER EIGHTEEN

Einri takes some convincing before it lets Waren dock the *Mouse* in *Nova's* hold, but soon enough we're all drifting together, all except Mookie.

I take Mookie's kit from the medbay into the mess hall, where Squid left Seven's body wrapped in an old piece of linen—maybe a pillowcase. Squid and Trix sit at the opposite end of the table from Seven, drinking ersatz coffee.

"The boy is still in the autodoc," Squid says when they see me come in. "Maybe if Mookie was here he could do more, but I think for now we need to let him rest and heal. There's no way of knowing how he'll react to life outside the box."

Trix reaches across the table and rests her natural hand on Squid's arm. "You've done all you can for the boy." Einri has already fabricated her a new prosthetic, and she keeps those new fingers wrapped around her coffee mug.

I put Mookie's medkit down next to the bundle of Seven and take out a scalpel. I unfold the stained white cloth, and Squid walks over, announced by quiet footfalls and the smell of coffee. "Mars, what are you doing? She's dead."

"She's not dead," I say. I put the blade against Seven's sternum and softly thump the end of the handle to crack the thin bone. A minute later and Seven's shattered body sits open in front of me while Squid watches.

"Look," I say, and I hold up the "egg." It's perfectly round, with a transparent shell revealing whorls of pink within. "I told you Seven was an experiment. She carries her own clone around inside her." Squid leans forward, and I wipe the last of the blood off the shell.

They stare wide-eyed at the tiny pink fetus.

"Squid, meet Eight."

"That's incredible, but I'm not sure about 'Eight.' What about 'Ocho'?"

I smile. "I like that."

I wash my hands and then the egg and put it in the hood of my cloak, which will keep the egg warm and act like a marsupial's pouch when she hatches.

"I'm sorry I snapped at you on the ship," I say. "But I can't lose her, I just fucking can't." My eyes sting and I can feel tears seeping into them, but I blink the moisture away. That little terror; I love her so much, and watching her die breaks my heart no matter how many times I see it.

"It's okay," Squid says, "I get it." Then, apropos of nothing, they hug me, tightly, for as long as it takes me to relax into it and hug them back. Being held like that, for the first time in too long, the tears come for real.

. . .

I sleep for a whole day. When I wake the migraine is still lingering.

I sit down at the mess-hall table, waiting for the others so we can start Squid's "family meeting." I get myself a coffee, activate the shard holding all the information I have on my father, and swipe to the holo-image. I can rotate it a little, see the shape of my father's head, see a snatch of the background behind him, but that's it. I can't make out where he is, and I don't know who took the picture. Part of me wants to think it was my mother. It's the only echo of her in my life—that and the fact that I was born.

A few minutes later Trix joins me, sitting at the far end of the table, silently glaring.

"Sorry I'm late," Squid says, coming through from the cockpit. They sit down and look at the shard.

"Who is that?" Squid asks.

"The asshole who sold me to MEPHISTO."

"Slaver?"

"Father."

Trix laughs at that, a single throaty *hah* that tells me everything I need to know about her own father.

"Where's he now?" Squid asks.

"I dunno," I say. "My sister Sera found some information on him—but I haven't looked yet. Maybe he's dead."

Trix taps her foot a few times, then looks up toward the ceiling when she says, "What's our first move?"

"We've been heading away from the debris field—"

"The Mars Xi Debris Field," Squid says. "It'll be marked on every navmap one day."

Einri doesn't skip a beat: "And we should leave this system as soon as possible. The area is about to be filled with imperial junkers and MEPHISTO reinforcements."

"I've got my stackhead contact searching for known military prisons, so once I've got a list, I'm going to go find Mookie. He wouldn't be in this shit without me, and I'm not going to let them kill him."

"You're not doing it without me," Trix says.

"You still want to be near me after seeing all that?" I say, and I hang my head and close my eyes. Behind my lids all I can see are boys: boys stuffed into electric coffins, boys crushed, boys killed. My vision is washed with red, blood-tinted.

After a moment I look up and Trix shrugs. "This isn't about you."

"You didn't do anything MEPHISTO didn't deserve,"

Squid says. "And it's Mookie; he's family."

"I can't ask you to do this with me. It's probably fucking suicide."

"You didn't ask," Squid says, and then they smile a pure, reckless smile.

"All right, then. We're really gonna do this," I say. "Waren, we don't have a location yet, but I'll trust you and Einri to take us someplace safe in the interim."

"Thank you, Mars," Waren says. "There are a few areas of the galaxy I've always wanted to visit."

"Let's get out of this system."

Squid heads to the cockpit while Trix goes toward the rear of the ship. I head back to my quarters and stand in front of the viewscreen. The gas giant and its two moons are far off in the distance now, tiny splashes of color against the black void. There's so much death behind us, drifting in space. In front of us? Who knows.

I take Ocho's egg from my hood and hold it close to my lips. "I miss you already, jerkface."

Einri takes us into worm-space, and I watch as the whole universe folds down into nothingness.

We move on. We disappear.

Acknowledgments

Special thanks to Bryony Milner for her invaluable feedback, her friendship, and the Scotch. Thanks also to Austin Armatys for his feedback and enthusiasm, and Marlee Jane Ward for all her support. Thank you to Carl Engle-Laird for his detailed and thoughtful editorial feedback and for taking a chance on *Killing Gravity* in the first place.

Finally, thanks to These Arms Are Snakes and Genghis Tron, whose music informed aspects of this story.

About the Author

Photograph by Marlee Jane Ward

Corey J. White is a writer of science fiction, horror, magical realism, and other, harder to define stories. He studied writing at Griffith University, and is now based in Melbourne. *Killing Gravity* is his first book.

Find him at coreyjwhite.com and on twitter at @cjwhite.

TOR·COM

Science fiction. Fantasy. The universe.

And related subjects.

*

More than just a publisher's website, *Tor.com* is a venue for **original fiction, comics,** and **discussion** of the entire field of SF and fantasy, in all media and from all sources. Visit our site today—and join the conversation yourself.